BACHELOR'S BAIT

COCKTALES
BOOK 3

MARI CARR

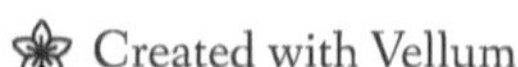 Created with Vellum

BACHELOR'S BAIT

Sophie doesn't feel the need to explain herself to anyone, least of all the free-aid lawyer who's determined to judge her as a society princess. She'd ignore him altogether...if he weren't so damn hot and didn't make her want such dirty, naughty things.

Marc has no time for Sophie's bachelor auction and he certainly doesn't want to be trapped in the web of a spoiled brat. Problem is the more he gets to know Sophie, the more he wants her...in his bed, over his lap, against a wall.

This story is dedicated to Deb. A great basketball coach and an even better friend.

BACHELOR'S BAIT

1 1/2 oz. gin
1 dash orange bitters
1/2 tsp. grenadine
White of one egg

Shake and strain into 4 oz. cocktail glass.

CHAPTER ONE

Sophie Kennedy dashed out of the manicurist's shop feeling like a jackass. She was barefoot with cotton stuffed between each of her toes, thanks to her unfinished pedicure. She glanced left then right, trying to recall which direction Patricia Butler–Baines had gone.

"No good deed goes unpunished," she muttered under her breath, mentally flipping a coin and heading to the right. She lifted her iPhone and awkwardly tried to find Patricia's name in her list of contacts. God knew it would be an easier task if she wasn't running with a freaking toy poodle named Pookie in the bag hanging over her shoulder.

Patricia, one of the most annoying women in the world, had spotted her while Sophie was getting the pedicure. Sophie had just dipped her feet into the cool soaking solution and closed her eyes, grateful for a few minutes of relaxing quiet. That quiet had lasted exactly twenty-four seconds before Patricia burst into the shop. She'd made a beeline straight for Sophie, giving her an earful about everything that was going wrong with the huge birthday bash Patricia was throwing for herself.

Sophie had listened with a sympathetic ear—since she certainly couldn't get a word in edgewise—to Patricia's ridiculously long tale of woe. The highlights included the caterer quitting at the last minute (who could blame him), the rental company daring to deliver a tent that wasn't completely pristine white (apparently there were two dark smudges on one hem) and the florist failing to find hydrangeas that exactly matched the color of Patricia's eyes.

Sweet Jesus. *Really?*

Desperate for silence, Sophie had foolishly agreed to speak to another caterer on Patricia's behalf. She'd suggested someone try soap and water to get the smudges out of the tent. Finally, she assured the woman that nature could never hope to capture the beauty of her eyes, and it was foolish to even try to find flowers that matched. As Sophie expected, Patricia's vanity was sufficiently stroked by the compliment. Not that it mattered to Sophie. She was just hoping to give the florist a break from the insanity.

Patricia, appeased, left with as much fanfare as she'd entered, waving to acquaintances and oohing and aahing loudly over some new shade of nail polish, assuming everyone in the place would want to know her opinion. It wasn't until the pedicurist came over, dried Sophie's feet and began to apply the polish that they noticed Pookie whimpering in her case.

"That dog needs to pee," the woman stated matter-of-factly.

Sophie agreed.

"You'd better find the lady and give her back her dog."

So now Sophie was rushing barefoot down the sidewalk with a freaking dog in a purse, trying to text Patricia, the last person on Earth she wanted to see for even three more seconds today.

She picked up her pace when she thought she saw the back of Patricia's blonde head turning a corner ahead. Sophie was texting the word "wait" when she was knocked roughly off-balance.

She juggled her cell phone for a few seconds before giving up as Pookie began sliding off her shoulder. The man she'd collided with dropped the files he'd been carrying, papers flying everywhere. His phone hit the sidewalk next to hers.

"Shit!" they cried in unison.

Sophie hastily knelt to help him save the papers as a breeze threatened to blow them all away.

"Hasn't anyone ever told you about the dangers of texting and walking?" he asked angrily.

Sophie was in no mood to be chastised by anyone. "Hasn't anyone ever told *you* to look both ways before crossing the street?"

"This is a sidewalk."

"Same difference." She stuffed the papers she'd recovered into a file folder. "Dammit," she said as she handed it to him.

"What's wrong?" he asked.

"I broke a nail." She hadn't even paid for the freaking manicure yet.

"Sorry to hear that, princess."

His sardonic tone was the last straw.

Sophie narrowed her eyes. "Is sarcasm your first language or are you bilingual?"

Before the man could answer, Pookie wiggled free from the case, walked toward the building the man had just exited, lifted her leg and peed.

Sophie giggled when the man scowled. "Your dog is pissing on my office door."

She shrugged. "So sue me."

The man's face instantly morphed into a grin Sophie didn't trust. He raised his finger, pointing to the sign on the window.

Market Street Free Legal Aid, Marc Garrett, Attorney at Law.

Sophie grabbed her phone, stuffing it in her back jeans pocket as she stood. Her manicure was ruined, her relaxing pedicure over and she still had the damn dog in her possession. She returned his smile as she picked up Pookie and returned her to the case. "My name is Patricia Butler–Baines. Do your worst."

"Don't tempt me," he said before she could get out of earshot.

Turning, she headed toward The Nail Gallery without a backward glance. The man—Marc, she assumed—didn't bother to follow her.

She tried to ignore the odd part of her that was strangely disappointed. Asshole or not, he was pretty freaking hot. She blew out a long breath and shook off the feeling. The guy was a prick, and chances were good she'd never see him again.

Good riddance.

When she returned to the shop, she opened the door to discover Patricia waiting for her.

"Pookie!" Patricia cried, acting as if Sophie had kidnapped the silly mutt. Pookie barked as she was returned to her owner. Patricia, in true dramatic fashion, snuggled and kissed the dog as though they'd been separated for years rather than twenty minutes.

The mani-pedi Sophie had allotted sixty minutes for actually ate up two hours of her afternoon, since she'd essentially had to start over. By the time she dragged herself into Books and Brew for work, she was done in.

"You're late," Stephanie called out from behind the bar.

"Bite me." Sophie walked straight to the storeroom to stash her purse. She was part owner of the bookstore-slash-bar with her three best friends, Stephanie, Jordan and Jayne. They were closer than sisters. Therefore the need to mince words and pretend to play nice had disappeared long ago.

"I tried to call you a couple times," Stephanie said while Sophie grabbed an apron.

Sophie frowned and reached into her pocket to pull out her cell. "My phone never rang."

"I know. That's because you currently don't *have* your phone."

The second Sophie saw it she knew Stephanie was telling the truth. She'd picked up the asshole's phone instead of her own. "Shit."

"That's what the guy who answered *your* phone said. Mr. Garrett is coming by tonight to make the switch with you."

"You told him where to find me?"

Stephanie frowned. "I figured you'd want your phone back. Who is this guy? And why did you tell him your name is Patricia Butt–Bitch?" Stephanie never called Patricia by her given name.

Sophie sighed. "Nobody. Just some guy I ran into on the sidewalk."

Literally.

"He sounded nice enough to me, though a bit frustrated with the phone mix-up. What's his problem? Nerdy? Annoying?"

"Asshole," Sophie supplied easily, though she wasn't sure it was fair to keep labeling him as such, given they'd only talked a couple of minutes at most.

"Ah. If you want to hide in the back when he gets here, I can make the swap for you. Unfortunately, I don't know exactly what time he's coming. Said something about stopping by after a meeting with a judge. You think he's in trouble with the law? Wonder what he did."

"He's a free-aid lawyer. His office is near The Nail Gallery."

"Oh. Well, he can't be all bad then, can he? I mean, rather than using his law degree to make a bundle of cash, he's putting his talents to use to help the less fortunate. Jared said those free legal aid clinics do some really good things for domestic violence victims and the community as a whole."

Stephanie, who served as the bartender at Books and Brew, had recently fallen head over heels for Jared, a local cop. The woman who'd always sworn off relationships had been bitten hard by the love bug, and Sophie couldn't be happier for her.

Sophie found her first impression of Marc wavering in the face of Stephanie's argument. Before she could admit it, the phone in her hand started ringing. Justin Timberlake's SNL song "Dick in a Box" sounded loud enough that everyone in the place turned to look at her, then laughed.

"Ugh," she groaned. "See?" She gestured to the phone as Stephanie grinned widely. "Asshole."

Sophie answered the phone when she saw her own cell number on the screen. "'Dick in a Box'? Really? What's wrong with you?"

Marc laughed on the other end. "It's called humor, Sophie. You should give it a try."

She forced herself to take a deep breath—then realized he'd called her by her real name. "Stephanie told you who I was."

"I knew who you were the second I saw you on the side-walk. Sort of hard not to recognize one of society's darlings. Your picture's in the paper all the time."

She noticed a distinct tone of disdain in his voice. Unfortunately, she couldn't refute that statement. He was right. Her father was one of the wealthiest businessmen in the state. A widower, he often looked to Sophie, his only daughter, to serve as hostess for his high-society shindigs. Jasper Kennedy did nothing in half measures, so as a result, the press often covered his black-tie affairs with rabid interests, the public dying to see how he would top himself with each event.

"When are you coming by? I need my phone."

"I'll be stuck in this meeting for a little while longer. We're on a short break because the judge needed to look over some paperwork. I wanted to see how long you planned to hang out at that bar."

"I'm not hanging out. I work here."

Silence met her from the other end of the line. Sophie took a sick sense of pride in shocking the attorney. He clearly thought he had her figured out, placing her in the high-society-bitch category along with the Patricia Butler–Baineses of the world.

"You work in a bar?" he finally asked.

"Yep. Waiting tables tonight until close."

"You're a *waitress?*"

She didn't bother to explain she was part owner. She sort of liked keeping the cocky man in a state of ignorance. It felt good to shatter his preconceived illusions.

Sophie herself was actually struggling to find an identity that fit, though she'd certainly never admit it to Marc Garrett. She knew she didn't want to live in her father's world, hanging out at the country club and attending benefits and balls with the sole purpose of becoming someone's trophy wife, but at the same time, she certainly hadn't intended to wait tables for the rest of her life.

She'd always thought she'd put her bachelor's degree in marketing to work, making Books and Brew a huge success. Sadly, those skills seemed to be more useful to her father and his big parties. She didn't bring much more to the business she shared with her friends than serving drinks. Sophie was anxious to change that...somehow.

She wanted to be successful, wanted her life to serve some purpose. As to what that purpose should be, she didn't have a clue. But for now...

"Yes, Marc. I'm a waitress. Do you have a problem with that?"

"No. No problem. Just trying to figure out why. Your father has more money than God. Why the hell do you need to work for minimum wage and tips? Daddy not footing the bill for your pedicures?"

"Are you always this rude?"

"Sweetheart, you've caught me on a good day. I haven't even started to be rude yet."

"That sounds like my cue to hang up. See you later."

She clicked off before Marc could say anything else. She felt a sense of accomplishment in getting the last word. No doubt that was something Marc took pride in achieving more often than not.

The phone rang again, the damn "Dick in a Box" song blasting through the bar. Her own number taunted her once more. While she wanted to ignore the call, she wanted to make the song end just as quickly.

"What?" she said into the receiver.

"It's rude to hang up on someone."

As if to prove his point, Marc did just that, the phone going dead before she could issue a retort.

"*Asshole,*" she muttered. She silenced the phone and shoved it in her pocket, trying to push Marc Garrett's face and voice from her mind.

That was easier said than done. If work had been even the slightest bit busy, she'd have been able to keep from thinking about the handsome, infuriating lawyer's blue eyes. She wouldn't have had so many hours to consider the muscular arms his dress shirt couldn't conceal.

Instead, the afternoon trudged by at a snail's pace, offering her too much time to fantasize. Typically Thursday was a busy day for them, what with Jayne's Romantic Hearts book club normally filling the seating area of the bar for their discussion, but the group had taken a hiatus this week since tomorrow was the Fourth of July. Many of the book group members were mothers with small children, so they'd be preparing for picnics and fireworks or heading out of town for the holiday weekend.

Jayne sat at the end of the bar looking as tired as Sophie felt. "Why don't you go home, Jayne? You've had a hell of a day." Jayne volunteered at the local library. She'd spent the morning helping with an Independence Day party for local preschoolers, dressing up in red, white and blue, reading history-themed children's books and serving cookies in the shape of the American flag. According to Jayne, the party had been a big, noisy success.

Jayne stifled a yawn. "I'm too tired to move off this stool to make the trek home. Remind me again why we didn't close for the holiday?"

Stephanie busied herself wiping glasses, hanging them on the rack behind the bar. "Because this place will fill up later tonight when folks shake off work and get ready to celebrate the long weekend. Don't you remember last year? The bar was packed. It was one of our best nights all year, profit-wise."

Sophie nodded. "Yep. She's right. This is the calm before the storm. No one will be here until after dark."

Jayne sighed. "Then I probably shouldn't go home. You'll need me later."

Stephanie shrugged. "It's not even five yet. What if you go home for a few hours, put your feet up and come back to work until close? Sophie and I can handle things until then. Jordan said she'd be back at eight to help with the holiday partiers."

The beauty of owning their own business was the ability

to come and go as they wanted. Jordan worked the most conventional hours of the four, opting to do her bookkeeper and office manager duties during the traditional nine-to-five workday. However, on nights as busy as tonight was likely to be, she'd help wait tables or man the cash register on the bookstore side.

Stephanie, the night owl, loved working the late shift, not willing to give up her morning sleep-ins. Sophie and Jayne sort of made up the rest of the time, sometimes coming in early, other days working the later hours. They'd agreed to commit three years to building the business and growing a decent profit before they considered hiring full-time help.

So far they'd been able to keep things rolling on their own, but it had impacted their social lives. Stephanie was the only one of the four with a boyfriend, but as a detective, Jared's hours were as odd as Stephanie's. Somehow they managed to make it work, living together and designating Wednesdays as their "date night".

Sophie really didn't struggle too hard for dates. She had plenty of offers, and she accepted more often than not. The trick was finding a guy she wanted to go on a *second* date with. Her father tended to be the driving force behind her offers, introducing her to doctors and businessmen who ran in his social circles. Dad was determined to find her a "good husband". She played the dutiful daughter and honestly gave the men a fair shot. Unfortunately, her idea of the perfect man and her father's were as similar as thoroughbred horses and pack mules.

She didn't want a man whose singular goal was to acquire as much money and power as possible. She wanted a man with a career that wasn't the sole focus of his life, who'd come home at a reasonable hour, who wanted to have a family he'd be around to help raise.

While Sophie loved her father, it was her mother who'd done the lion's share of parenting when she was younger. Her mother, the sweetest woman to ever walk the planet, had been killed by a drunk driver when Sophie was thirteen and, at that point, Dad apparently decided she was old enough to finish the child-rearing by herself. He gave her everything she needed—a roof over her head, stylish clothing, a good education, birthday gifts galore and even a fancy sports car. The only thing he'd never seemed able to spare was time.

There was no way Sophie would let her own children grow up with a part-time father. She knew from firsthand experience, it sucked.

"Earth to Soph." Stephanie waved her hand in front of Sophie's face. She jerked herself out of her thoughts and back to the conversation at hand. "What's up with you today? You keep zoning out."

Sophie shrugged, picking up the beer their lone patron had ordered. "Just tired, I guess." She spun to deliver the drink—and ran straight into Marc.

The beer she was carrying splashed up and out of the glass like a mini geyser, covering them both in foamy suds.

"Why are you always in my way?" she snapped, looking at her drenched T-shirt.

Marc frowned, swiping at the beer covering his dress shirt. "Why are you always rushing everywhere without looking where you're going?"

Stephanie stepped between them with a couple of bar

towels. "I take it this is the cell guy. I'm Stephanie. We spoke earlier."

Marc accepted her offer of a towel with a friendly smile. Sophie tried to ignore the fact that all she'd managed to get from the man were smirks and scowls.

"Marc Garrett."

"I'm Jayne." Jayne gave him a quick wave as she produced a mop to clean up the floor.

"There's a bathroom down that hall," Stephanie said, gesturing toward the back. She returned to the bar and grabbed a Books and Brew T-shirt, handing it to him. "Here. It's nice and dry. At least until Sophie bumps into you again."

"You're hilarious, Steph." Sophie grabbed another one of the clean T-shirts for herself then gestured for Marc to follow. Despite the fact he was soaked in beer, he didn't seem as annoyed as he had when they'd collided on the street.

She pointed to a door. "That's the men's room. You can change in there."

"Thanks." He entered the room, the door closing behind him.

Sophie tried to shake from her mind the image of his shirt clinging to some fairly impressive pecs. What was wrong with her today? While her libido was far from inactive, something about the cocky lawyer set it off in grand style.

She walked into the ladies' room and stripped off her wet shirt. Grabbing some paper towels, she dampened them and tried to wash away the smell of beer from her skin. Luckily the shirt had soaked up most of the liquid, so her bra was fairly dry. Tugging the new shirt over her head, she splashed some cold water on her cheeks and returned to the hallway. She'd only taken a few steps when Marc's head poked out of the doorway. He didn't bother to leave the men's room.

"What are you doing?" she asked.

He gave her shit-eating grin. "Making sure the coast is clear. Trying to avoid being run over by the society princess for a third time today."

She narrowed her eyes. "You're an idiot."

He joined her in the hall. "Aw, Soph. That hurts."

She tried to tell herself she didn't like him using the nickname generally reserved for her best friends. She reached into her pocket and pulled out his phone. "Here. Let's make the swap and then you can be on your way. I'm sure there must be a list of women a mile long hoping to spend the evening with a guy like you."

"Like me?"

"One who fairly oozes with charming wit."

"Oh. I'm *that* man, am I?" He took his phone but made no move to return hers, even though her hand remained outstretched.

"Aren't you forgetting something?" she asked.

He shook his head. "The night's young and it doesn't look very busy here. I've had a hell of a day. I was thinking I might stick around for a drink."

Sophie tried to ignore the way her body heated under his rather sexy perusal of her. "Fine. You can just sit anywhere and I'll—"

"I was hoping you'd join me."

"Why on earth would I want to have a drink with you?"

"Why wouldn't you?"

Sophie's eyebrows lifted. "Should I make a list?"

He grasped her hand, forcing her to shake his. "Let's start over. I'm Marc Garrett. And you are?"

"Sophie Kennedy."

"Sophie. I've had a very long, rather painful day thanks to you and your father. The least you could do is have a drink with me."

She dropped his hand. "What does my dad have to do with anything?"

He tilted his head, and she got the impression he was trying to read something in her face. "Nothing, apparently."

Once more he took her hand, but this time he used it to tug her toward a corner table. Stephanie had poured and delivered a new beer to their only customer. It appeared Jayne had decided to go home for a brief respite after all.

Stephanie came over as soon as they sat down. "Aw. This is sweet. You two decided to play nice. You want something to drink, Marc?"

He nodded. "I'd love a Heineken. What about you, Sophie? My treat."

"I'm working."

Stephanie scoffed. "Like that's ever stopped us from having a cold one on slow afternoons. I'll get you your usual."

Stephanie returned to the bar to get their drinks.

"What's your usual?"

She didn't want to say, afraid Marc would read too much into it. Of course, her silence didn't matter when Stephanie returned to the table and placed two bottles of Heineken and frosty mugs in front of them.

"On the house," Stephanie said before returning to the bar.

Marc raised his eyebrows when he saw her beer of

choice. He lifted his bottle and tapped it against hers. "To good taste."

She acknowledged his toast with a slight nod then took a sip of the cool brew. It went down far too easy after the crazy day she'd had. Her long sigh must have given that away.

"Sounds like you've had a day and a half too." If she'd thought Marc was handsome when he was frowning, his face now—as he offered a friendly smile—was drop-dead gorgeous.

She nodded. "It's been an interesting one." It had started with an early phone call from her father, asking how his latest attempt at matchmaking had fared. She'd lied, telling Dad his golfing buddy—a world-renowned neurosurgeon— was very nice. In reality, the man had bored her to tears over the pre-dinner drinks and appetizer, spent most of the main course on the phone conferring about a patient then tried to grope her during dessert. Hell would freeze over before she'd consent to another date, but she hadn't confessed as much to her father. Better to play the duck-and-dodge game, avoiding phone calls and making up excuses until the guy stopped calling.

She'd become a master at giving the illusion of being "interested but busy".

"You don't have plans for the holiday?" Marc took another drink of his beer.

She shook her head. If Stephanie hadn't said something earlier, she would have forgotten all about the Fourth of July. "Nope. Just work. I know it doesn't look like it now, but we'll actually do very good business later as folks roll in to kick off the holiday."

"I imagine you will. You're in the perfect part of town for

a business like this. So how is it a debutante such as yourself ended up waiting tables in a bar?"

Sophie's temper spiked. "It's amazing how you can irritate me with just one question. Number one, I'm not a debutante. Number two—and not that it's any of your damn business—I'm part owner of this place. In addition to waiting tables and helping out on the bookstore side, I'm in charge of marketing and special events."

"Ah. So you plan parties for a living. Now it's all starting to make sense."

Sophie narrowed her eyes. "Did I do something to piss you off? Something more than bumping into you a couple times?"

Marc leaned back and released a long breath. "I think it's your name that gets under my skin. You're not exactly what I was expecting after reading about you in the society pages and knowing who your father is."

"Again with my father. What do you have against him?"

Marc didn't reply immediately, and again she was struck by the feeling he was sizing her up, trying to decide something, though she didn't have a clue what that could be.

Finally, he said, "I sort of thought you ran into me on purpose today."

She frowned. "Why the hell would I do that?"

"I was late for an important meeting. With your father's lawyers and a judge."

Sophie knew very little about her father's business, but it was obvious Marc didn't realize that. Dad's sole use for her was for entertaining purposes. He didn't think she was interested in learning the details of his professional life. At least, she told herself he assumed a lack of interest. It was simply too painful to consider the idea that he felt her intelligence was deficient.

"Are you suing my father?"

He shook his head. "Not exactly. I'm fighting to save something your father doesn't want saved."

"What?"

Marc didn't reply. Instead, he changed the subject. "So you're part owner of Books and Brew?" He looked around the room, nodding approvingly. "It's a cool place. I've walked by here a few times but I've never come in. I'm sorry about that now. I love the idea of booze and books."

His impressed assessment only partially appeased her curiosity. What the hell was up between Dad and Marc? Rather than call him on it, she let his dodge stick. "The bar part was Stephanie's idea. She said if she was going to a bookstore, she preferred to drink a cold beer or a glass of wine rather than a cup of damn coffee."

"Stephanie's very wise," Marc joked.

"She has her moments. Few and far between though they may be. She and I were roommates in college. Jordan and Jayne, the other partners, were our suitemates. After two years in the dorm, the four of us found an apartment off campus for our junior and senior terms. We were only a few weeks away from graduation when we came up with the idea for this place. It took a few years of saving and scrambling to get the investment money, but with the four of us pooling our resources, it worked out eventually. Jayne's parents helped her. Jordan and Stephanie saved up some of the capital then managed to get small-business loans. My mother left me money in her will, a small trust fund that I invested in the business."

Marc listened intently as she spoke, and Sophie wondered why she was sharing so much. The man confused her, left her hot and bothered, trying to decide if she was mad or horny.

She cleared her throat. "Well, long story short—too late, right?—we all committed to three years of making the place a success, and that means working holidays, waiting tables, stocking shelves and playing busboy."

Marc tipped his bottle, finishing the beer before putting it back on the table. "Sounds like you're off to a great start. Color me impressed."

"So enough of the stalling. Why are you and my dear old dad at odds?"

Marc frowned. "He's trying to close down the community center."

His response knocked Sophie off guard. "No," she said, more to herself than to Marc. She looked at the attorney and shook her head. "No. My dad wouldn't do that."

Her mother had taken her to dance classes and piano lessons at the community center when she was younger. The place was an institution in the city—a gathering place for senior citizens and a safe harbor for latchkey kids, after school and in the summer. It offered classes in everything from knitting to ballroom dancing. Her mother had served on the board for years, keeping the center running by planning some of the programs and helping to raise funds to keep it solvent.

Dad knew how much the place had meant to her mother...and to Sophie. He'd never allow it to close.

Marc didn't respond, but she sensed her face had

answered an unspoken question for him. "You really didn't know?"

She shook her head again. "I didn't know because it's not happening. You're wrong."

Marc tapped his fingers on the table lightly, the sound of the fast rhythm capturing her attention. It made her realize her own nervous habit—bouncing her leg whenever she was stressed out—was commencing full speed beneath the table. She forced herself to still the motion.

Again, she got a sense he was trying to make a decision about her. "It's not exactly common knowledge yet. It hasn't hit the papers or anything. I was approached a few weeks ago by the chairman of the board of trustees at the center, Rich Gregory. There had been some anonymous inquiries in regards to the condition of the building over the past year. As a result, the center was subjected to a visit from the building inspector and threatened with some hefty fines if they didn't make repairs."

"It's an old building—" she started, but Marc continued.

"Then there was an audit of the books after someone sent a letter to the IRS, alleging that the trustees were misappropriating funds. They weren't, of course, but getting all the files in order has been time-consuming and costly. Rich came to me because he's afraid someone is trying to sabotage the center. Paying the accounting firm for help on the audit has left the center strapped for cash. The money to make the repairs needed to keep the building open isn't there."

Sophie didn't like the accusation Marc was making. "None of this implicates my father. All the complaints lodged were anonymous. It's pretty ballsy of you to accuse my dad with no more proof than—"

"A few weeks ago, your dad made the center an offer," Marc interrupted.

"An offer or a donation?" Sophie knew for a fact her father had contributed huge amounts of money to the center in the past. Clearly Marc and Rich were misreading the situation. Looking for a villain.

"It was an *offer*, Sophie. He wants to buy the property. At first, Rich was hopeful that your dad was planning to purchase the center with the intention of improving the place. He thought Jasper was digging them out of their hole. After the string of bad luck and growing debt, the idea of privatizing the center had almost seemed like the answer to a prayer for the trustees. The center is in big trouble financially."

"So my dad's offer is a good one. He'll buy the center and fix it up, make it better than ever."

It was Marc's turn to shake his head. "Rich caught wind of your dad's plans. He has a friend on the zoning committee who learned Jasper was interested in acquiring the property for a more profitable purpose. He intends to tear the center down and build a shopping mall. That's when Rich called me."

Sophie's temper snapped. "No. Dad would never do that. How can you sit here and spread gossip around like it's the gospel truth? This is slander! It's unfair and—"

"Your father's lawyers confirmed today that was indeed the plan."

He had a bad habit of interrupting her. Sophie's face flushed with anger and frustration.

Marc leaned forward. She tried to ignore the almost

sympathetic look in his eyes. How dare he sit there and spew lie after lie then act as if he felt *sorry* for her!

"The community center has sixty days to come up with the money to make the repairs or they'll be forced to close their doors. And with the bad building inspection hanging over their heads, the trustees will be forced to accept your dad's offer, which is less than generous. I think your father actually feels like he's doing the community a service by taking the 'eyesore' off their hands and replacing it with something new and shiny."

Sophie swallowed heavily, desperate to prove her father's innocence. Unfortunately, Marc's last comment triggered a memory. Dad had once bought some riverfront property, tearing down the beautiful homes that had stood there for well over a hundred years to build a new subdivision full of McMansions. He'd called the old homes "eyesores", an affront to people with good taste.

The comment had actually led to a huge disagreement between them—something they rarely had. Eventually she'd given up the fight, deciding it wasn't important. Once her father set his mind on a goal, he pursued it with the force of a two-ton tank, and it was clear her opinion wouldn't sway him.

But the community center was different. They hadn't lived in the riverfront homes, so she'd had no personal attachment to them. Her mother had given countless hours to the center, and it had played a major role in Sophie's happy memories of childhood. She loved the place dearly—and her father knew it.

It wasn't an eyesore. It was as necessary to the city as clean water, sanitation and fresh air.

"Soph?" Marc prodded when the silence between them lasted too long.

"My name is Sophia. And you're wrong about all of this." Her tone was biting, bitchy. There was a lump in her throat, and she was fighting desperately to keep her eyes dry when all she wanted to do was cry. "I think you should leave."

Marc nodded, rising slowly. He took her phone out of his pocket and placed it on the table. "I hope I *am* wrong. Good-bye, Sophie."

Marc left the bar. Once again he'd gotten the last word, but Sophie was suddenly too exhausted to give a shit.

Her long day had officially given way to an endless evening.

CHAPTER TWO

S ophie cursed her shoe choice. While she was no stranger to high heels, she'd misjudged exactly how much time she'd be on her feet tonight. Usually she had her shit together when it came to the charity events she helped organize, but the last week had been particularly rough.

Her father had gone out of the country the morning after her conversation with Marc about the community center. She'd tried to call Dad several times, but between the time change and his business meetings, she kept getting his voicemail.

On top of her concerns regarding the center, her girlfriend Jordan had chosen the past week to dive back into the dating world after a very long hiatus. Much to Sophie's delight, her friend had sparked the interest of two different guys. While Sophie was thrilled that Jordan was having such good fortune on the dating front, she couldn't help but feel a twinge of jealousy. The lucky bitch had two guys fighting for her attention while Sophie was experiencing a long, painful string of bad first dates.

Getting laid would go a long way toward relieving some of her pent-up stress. Her vibrator was no longer cutting it.

Unfortunately, the only man who even remotely interested her sexually was Marc, the obnoxious lawyer.

Sophie had never laid eyes on the man before plowing into him on the sidewalk last week, but now it seemed she couldn't turn around twice without seeing him.

Even though he continually pissed her off, she couldn't stop thinking about him in an entirely inappropriate, completely sexual way. Despite his ability to annoy her, she couldn't deny he was fucking hot, and there seemed to be some sort of dirty chemistry between them.

A couple days after their run-in at Books and Brew, she'd wound up in line behind him at the grocery store. They'd almost managed to feign politeness, talking about the hot weather and the city's fireworks display. But the way Marc had undressed her with his eyes, giving her a far-too-seductive look as he admired her cut-off jean shorts and tank top, had tweaked her libido *and* her temper. While their words were innocuous, the conversation drove her mind down naughty paths as she considered the explosive heat the two of them could generate between the sheets.

Then she'd run into him last night at Patricia Butt–Bitch's birthday party—the last place on Earth she'd ever expected to see him. Apparently he and Patricia's brother had gone to law school together. As luck would have it, Marc had been seated next to her. He'd muttered inappropriate though admittedly hilarious comments about the birthday girl and her guests all evening. There was no debating that his disregard for the country-club crowd was genuine.

She pretended to dislike Marc whenever she spoke to her friends about him, sticking by her assertion that he was an asshole. Though her body and mind seemed to be at odds. Despite disliking his abrasive personality, Sophie wanted him. Badly.

Yes, he was a jerk for accusing her father of such horrible things and for judging her for her place in Portland's social scene, but she still lusted after him. More than a few times his jokes had been laced with double meanings and sexual innuendoes. She'd been so frigging horny by the time she'd crawled into bed after the party, she'd tossed and turned all night.

Which was not helping her frame of mind right now. She was tired and on edge.

She headed toward the coat check to ask one of her volunteers, Charlotte, where she'd placed the box of extra flyers. Tonight's fundraiser was generating money for the domestic abuse shelter, and so far things were off to a great start. She was also happy to have one of her friends in attendance. Jordan had shown up on the arm of not just one of her suitors, but *both*. Sophie admired her friend's nerve and wondered which guy Jordan would ultimately choose, though she didn't envy her the decision. Both Gabriel and Casey were great catches. Sophie hadn't failed to notice the jealous looks Jordan was receiving from some of the single and even a few of the married women.

"Charlotte?" Sophie was annoyed to find the coat-check room unattended. She'd been an idiot to trust Charlotte to keep an eye on it. The woman was too flighty to take the task seriously. She was a regular at the bookstore, and when Sophie had foolishly mentioned her problem finding volunteers to help work the event, Charlotte had stepped forward. Sophie had accepted the offer, ignoring the voice telling her Charlotte only wanted to help so she could ogle the cream of society's crop in a glitzy setting.

Now she was staring at an unprotected room full of expensive shawls and jackets.

"Shit," she muttered. "Can anyone say *liability?*" She stepped behind the check-in counter and into the room, intent on finding the extra flyers. Then she'd track down her "volunteer" and read her the riot act for leaving her post unattended.

Spotting the box in a corner, she crossed the small space and bent to retrieve it.

A wolf whistle sounded from the doorway.

Sophie rose quickly but the damage was done. Clearly she'd given someone an eyeful of her ass wrapped in its tight skirt.

Marc leaned against the doorframe, looking far too pleased with the view she'd offered.

"Wow. Sexist much?"

He gave her a seductive grin. She wished her body would stop responding to him so forcefully. Her stomach clenched, her pussy dampened and she was grateful for the box in her hands or Marc would see them trembling.

He was unapologetic. "When I see something beautiful, I feel the need to appreciate it."

"And being the classy guy you are, you thought you'd whistle at me like a construction worker."

"I thought you might prefer *that* response over the first idea that popped into my head."

"Which was?"

"Stroking my hands over that gorgeous ass you just displayed for me."

The battle between Sophie's head and body flared. Her ass cheeks clenched, longing for that caress. Her less visceral side offered a reply. "Then you made the right call because I would have kneed you in the balls. Hard."

He nodded. "That's what I thought. Hence my whistle from all the way over here."

His tone was light and friendly, making it impossible to take offense at his comments. The closet wasn't that large, but his assessment was correct. Several feet protected his balls from her knee.

Sophie subtly pressed her legs together and tried to force air into her lungs. Apparently the space between them wasn't that safe after all. She flushed as her body heated at their proximity—and semi-privacy.

The observant man's dark-blue eyes narrowed.

He must be hell on juries. He notices far too much.

He stepped into the room. She tried to hide her shock when he closed the closet door behind him. The darkness was cut by a mellow glow provided by the low-watt fixture hanging in the center of the ceiling, and instantly she was reminded of nights spent beside a dying fire in her family's large living room. She was a sucker for a fireplace.

Marc's deep voice cut through the silence. "Maybe I was wrong."

Her eyes tried to adjust to the dim lighting as he continued to move closer. "About what?" Her throat tightened, making her words sound thick and far too loud in the small room.

Marc didn't answer immediately. Instead, he took the box of flyers out of her hands, setting it on the floor. "You know I'm going to start coming by the bar, right? I feel the need to become a regular."

"Why? You get some sick pleasure out of annoying me?"

He shook his head, his voice laced with humor. "No. That's just a bonus."

The answer was completely unsatisfactory, even though Sophie liked the idea of him stopping by. Despite her better judgment, she wanted to see him more too. "Then why?" she repeated.

"Because I'll want to do this again."

He leaned forward and kissed her.

The motion caught her unaware. Her body reacted instantly as his hands landed on her waist, pulling her close. Her breath seized, her body tingled in places she didn't want to acknowledge and her heart began to race. This wasn't good.

It was *great*.

His lips were soft but firm. He kissed like a man who was used to being in charge. He pressed harder, parting his lips and hers at the same time so his tongue could explore. She lifted her hands to his shoulders, her breasts brushing his chest. The action triggered a stronger response in Marc, who lifted one hand to her head, fingers tangling gently in her hair, directing her movements.

She felt the dampness between her legs give way to genuine wet heat. She tightened her grip on his shoulders, trying to get impossibly closer. Marc's hand at her waist dropped lower, sliding until he cupped the ass he'd been admiring earlier.

The touch sparked two reactions in Sophie—full-fledged arousal and eye-opening comprehension of exactly what she was doing. The alarm began to sound, and her brain defeated her physical urge to strip them both naked, drag him to the floor and—

She pushed him away, struggling to catch her breath and still her pounding heart.

Marc released her, and her body screamed out in anger at his easy capitulation.

"You have some nerve," she said, hating the breathless quality in her voice.

He grinned, his face completely devoid of remorse. "You liked kissing me."

"You caught me by surprise."

He smoothed his hand along her cheek. It was a gentle touch with more physical impact than if he'd shoved those same gorgeous fingers inside her empty pussy.

"The evidence is indisputable. Surprise lasts for a few seconds at most. You let me kiss you for several minutes."

Freaking lawyers.

Time to retreat. Regroup.

"Whatever." Christ. That was it? That was her big, witty comeback? She needed to get her head screwed on straight because she was definitely losing her edge.

Stepping to the side, she walked around him toward the door. Once again, she was disappointed when he didn't try to stop her. Jesus. This was bad. Really bad.

She reached for the knob at the exact moment Marc's hand landed on the door, holding it closed. Her body shifted into overdrive at the power play. Since when was she turned on by shit like this? Usually she was the aggressor in her relationships, the top dog.

She spun to face Marc, refusing to let him think she was weak. "Careful, counselor. I'm still mad at you for your false accusations toward my dad and, despite my earlier surprise, I think you may find me *way* out of your league." She tried to sound intimidating, unafraid, but she feared she fell short of the mark.

Especially when Marc leaned forward. Sophie thought he was going to kiss her again. Her eyes actually started to drift shut in anticipation, but at the last minute he changed direction until his lips landed beside her ear. She tried to repress the shiver of charged excitement caused by his hot breath on her face. She was only half-successful and could picture Marc smirking at her primal response.

"Don't worry about me, princess. I know exactly what the outcome of this case will be. But by all means, keep proclaiming innocence if you want to. I like a challenge." He followed up his taunt with a sharp nip to her earlobe that should have infuriated her, but instead shot through her like molten lava.

She sucked in a deep breath, searching for a rebuttal. Her brain had gone on permanent vacation. Instead of speaking, she pushed him away with more force than was necessary and left the closet.

She reached the ballroom before she realized she'd forgotten the flyers.

And once again, she'd let him get the last word.

MARC WATCHED Sophie work the crowd, moving from table to table with grace and charm as she made certain each of the attendees had everything they needed to ensure they'd be not only happy, but generous as the evening progressed. He'd teased her about her job as a party planner, but he had to admit she had a flair for it. Not to mention the fact she was putting her talents to good use, raising money tonight for a cause that was quite close to his heart.

All his preconceived notions about the type of woman Sophie was were being destroyed, one after another.

After running into Ms. Kennedy outside his office last week, he'd done a bit of research on her.

His gut reaction when she'd plowed into him had been immediate suspicion. He wouldn't put it past Jasper Kennedy to use anything or anyone to achieve his goal of acquiring the community center property. Its location in the city made it a prime piece of real estate.

He had to hand it to Jasper. The man had connections to everyone. The meeting in the judge's chambers last week was a testament to that. It had been hastily arranged—the day before a *holiday*—no doubt to thwart the board of trustees' intention to fight against the sale of the center. As a result, Marc had been forced to stay up all night preparing the documents needed to give them time to raise the funds to make the building improvements.

Finding Sophie Kennedy outside his door just minutes before he'd been preparing to battle her father's lawyers had seemed far too coincidental.

However, fate had a perverse sense of humor. Especially when he'd discovered he had Sophie's phone. Sharing a drink with her at Books and Brew had at least convinced him

Jasper hadn't been using his daughter to prevent him from making it to the meeting on time. If anything, it appeared her father was hiding his plans from Sophie.

During their conversation last night at Patricia's birthday party, he'd learned she'd been unable to reach Jasper to question him, though she'd stuck to her assertion that her father was innocent of any wrongdoing. Marc briefly wondered if Jasper's leeriness over his daughter's response could somehow be used to the community center's benefit, but if so, he couldn't figure out how. Sophie refused to believe her dad was trying to close the center, and Jasper wasn't around to confirm or deny it either way. In the meantime, the hourglass was running out and the center was in trouble.

Marc wasn't sure why he kept making excuses to see Sophie. He'd pretended their grocery store run-in was a coincidence. Truth was, he had driven by the store as Sophie was walking in. And suddenly remembered that he needed milk. He'd turned his car around for an impromptu shopping excursion.

He didn't have such a handy excuse for attending Patricia's birthday party last night. When the brightly colored invitation had appeared in his mailbox a few weeks ago, he'd laughed out loud, tossed the thing aside and muttered something about hell freezing over before he went to the bash.

Next thing he knew, he'd found himself at the party and finagling a seat next to Sophie. Patricia had completely believed that he was hoping to chat with Ms. Kennedy in order to forge a business relationship with Jasper. Patricia— ever the social-climbing gossipmonger—had bought his story hook, line and sinker, and had been only too willing to change the table arrangements.

Marc was pleasantly surprised to discover how down-to-earth Sophie was. He'd assumed from the stories he'd read about her in the newspaper that she was another trophy-wife wannabe. He'd met enough of that type in his lifetime. It was one of the main reasons he'd walked away from a prosperous career in his family's law firm and moved all the way across the country. He'd wanted to escape his family's name and connections, to prove he could make it on his own.

He and Sophie had more in common than he'd let her believe. The Garretts were to DC what the Kennedys were to Portland. He'd left DC because he'd been working himself to death—and tired of fending off women who looked at him with dollar signs in their eyes, anxious to get a piece of the Garrett pie.

He'd expected Sophie to be shallow, more interested in her wardrobe than the needs of the community, but that wasn't the case. And while her trust was misplaced, he'd been touched by her loyalty to her father. He'd been even more impressed by her genuine concern for the center.

After his research, he was less surprised by Sophie's love for the place. He'd found several old pictures of her with her mother at community events and fundraisers. The center had clearly been an important part of her childhood and the relationship she'd shared with her mother, who had died when Sophie was a teenager.

Just seven days after running into her, Marc found himself knee-deep in an attraction he couldn't understand, didn't have time for, but wasn't willing to deny. Despite the fact his pursuit of her was a freaking gigantic conflict of interest. Jesus. He'd never put his cock ahead of his career, but with Sophie, he found his sense of professionalism wavering.

Sophia Kennedy was beautiful, sexy as sin and, more than that, she intrigued him, a trait that had been absent in his last few girlfriends.

He recalled her response to him in the coat closet. He wasn't sure what had prompted him to kiss her, but something in her face had told him she was equally aware of the chemistry between them.

Sophie continued to make her way around the room, stopping at Gabriel Lawson's table to talk to the woman sitting there. He'd heard through the grapevine that the wealthy bachelor was dating Jordan, the bookkeeper for Books and Brew. She was the only friend he hadn't met last week. The way they leaned closer, sharing confidences, indicated their friendship was as strong as those he'd observed between Sophie, Jayne and Stephanie.

Sophie had her back to him and seemed to be fixing her hair in a mirror, but he could tell she was really looking at him through the reflection. When Jordan's gaze found him as well, he knew they were talking about him.

He winked at Sophie, enjoying the way her shoulders stiffened just before she snapped the mirror shut and put it away. He was getting under her skin.

Now if only he could get under her clothes...

His gaze was broken when an acquaintance, Chuck Nelson, came over and stood next to him. "Damn monkey suit," Chuck muttered, tugging at his bow tie.

Marc gave him a companionable nod. While he didn't mind dressing up occasionally, he suspected Chuck's tux had fit better when he'd bought it. The obnoxious real estate agent had gained quite a few pounds in the past year or so.

Marc suspected if he looked up the word *blowhard* in the dictionary, he'd find a picture of Chuck. Nevertheless, it was a charity fundraiser, so Marc pasted on a false smile and pretended to share Chuck's derision for the formal attire. "I suppose the ladies like to see us dressed up, and since they're the ones putting on the shindig, they decide the dress code."

Chuck sighed heavily. "Yeah, I guess so, but just once I'd like to see the invitation for one of these damn events say it's okay to wear sweats and football jerseys."

Marc laughed, though he didn't relish the thought of seeing Chuck in sweatpants at some swanky restaurant. "You should pass that suggestion along to Sophie Kennedy. Isn't she behind the planning for most of these events?" Marc hoped Chuck would take him up on his suggestion, perfectly aware he was setting her up for his own personal entertainment. He'd love to see Sophie's face and hear her response to Chuck's inane wish.

"Not likely she'd listen to *me*," Chuck replied. "We dated a couple of years ago, you know."

Marc plastered a nonchalant expression on his face, though he couldn't imagine Sophie seriously being interested in the buffoon. "Is that so?"

"Yep." Chuck leaned closer and lowered his voice. "She broke up with me because I was too *big*. If you know what I mean."

Chuck gave him a cocky wink that had Marc's hand balling up in a fist. He wasn't sure exactly why he felt the urge to knock the guy on his ass, but it was pulsing strong and hard. He needed to put some distance between them.

"Excuse me, Chuck. I promised Mrs. Clarkson a dance."

"Oh yeah. Sure thing."

Chuck turned around to converse with another real estate agent who'd just joined them. Marc walked straight past the dance floor and outside to the patio, seeking some fresh air.

What the hell was wrong with him? He'd had a handful of conversations with Sophie, and they'd shared a single kiss —albeit a hot one—less than an hour ago. So why was he feeling jealous, almost possessive of her?

Shit, she was the type of woman he'd spent a lifetime trying to avoid. He didn't pursue country-club queens, and despite the fact Sophie owned and ran her own business, she was also a big part of the upper crust as well.

Not to mention he was currently the lawyer working to stop her father's purchase of the community center. Hell, as long as she continued to defend her father, she could technically be considered not just a conflict of interest, but an adversary.

He took a deep, steadying breath and forced himself to face the truth.

She'd never be his foe. And now that he thought about it, her past lovers didn't mean a damn thing, either. It was only her *future* partner he was interested in because he didn't have a doubt the next bed Sophie Kennedy slept in would be his. He wanted her. And despite the fact his attraction was dangerous and unbelievably stupid, he wasn't a man who denied himself what he wanted.

He took a few minutes to enjoy the quiet evening, letting his new reality sink in before rejoining the party.

The rest of the night passed quickly as he conversed with

several fellow lawyers over Scotch and sodas at the bar. Ordinarily he would have escaped the party shortly after dinner, but tonight he remained, content to chat and watch Sophie in her element.

As the gathering began to wind down, he offered to walk her to her car. "Thanks for attending."

"Anytime." He considered trying to steal another kiss, but Sophie anticipated the move. She claimed her seat behind the steering wheel so quickly she almost hit her head on the car door.

He resisted the urge to chuckle and call her coward.

"Well, good night." She slammed the door, clearly desperate to make her escape. He took a step away from the car but made no move to head to his truck across the parking lot. Truth be told, he needed her to drive away so he could adjust the hard-on residing in his pants. He'd risk an injury if he attempted walking with it in its current position.

Sophie turned the key—and nothing. The engine didn't fire. Twice more she twisted the key, but he could tell from the silence her battery was dead. Marc glanced around the parking lot. They were the last two guests to leave.

She wearily climbed out of the car. "I don't suppose you have jumper cables, do you? And if so, do you know how to use them?"

He shook his head. "I loaned my set to a client a few weeks ago. She hasn't returned them yet." He actually didn't expect to see them again at all. He'd planned to buy new ones. Unfortunately he hadn't had the time.

"Great."

"How about I give you a ride home? I'll buy some cables and pick you up in the morning. I can bring you back here and give you a jump before work." His cock thickened even more as he thought about exactly *how* he wanted to jump her.

"Oh, you don't have to go to all that trouble. I'll take you up on the ride home then figure out the jumper cables tomorrow. I'm sure Jared, Stephanie's boyfriend, has some."

He gestured toward his truck. "It's no trouble." Sophie walked toward his vehicle. He let her get a two-step lead before he did a quick pants adjustment and followed. He opened the passenger door, enjoying her impressed look at his chivalry.

"I'm not a total heathen."

She laughed softly. "I never said you were."

Marc climbed behind the steering wheel and started the car. The devil inside prompted him to tackle an issue that had been niggling at him all night, despite his mental pep talk. "So...you and Chuck Nelson were an item."

Sophie rolled her eyes. "Jesus. He never wastes much time spilling that tidbit. We dated for two months. It's a time I like to call my 'era of low self-esteem'. Fortunately it didn't take me too long to snap out of it and dump his ass."

Marc couldn't resist teasing her when he stopped at a red light. "According to Chuck, you dumped him because he was too big."

Sophie's jaw dropped.

He reached over, lightly closing her mouth. "Careful," he joked, "or you'll catch flies."

"He *said* that?" Her voice was filled with so much anger, he worried he may have to represent Sophie in court. Her face reflected pure murder.

"Sophie—" he began, wondering how to calm her down.

She cut him off. "I said he *was* the biggest dick, not he *had* the biggest dick."

"Oh well, that's an easy mistake to make," Marc teased.

"I think Chuck and I are going to have a little come-to-Jesus meeting tomorrow. There's no way I'm going to let him keep spreading that bullshit around. Goddamn pencil-dick ignoramus."

Marc laughed. "Remind me not to get on your bad side."

Sophie tilted her head, her anger dissipating quickly. "Since when have you ever been on anything *but* my bad side?"

"Aw, come on, Soph. You know you're hot for me."

She gave him a wicked grin. "Now that I think about it, you and Chuck have a lot in common."

He narrowed his eyes, unhappy about being compared to her idiot ex. "We have nothing in common and if you continue to insist we do, I'll be forced to prove just how different we are."

"Turn here. My house is the third one on the left," she said, as he approached her street. A successful dodge for Ms. Kennedy.

He pulled into her driveway. Again, he was taken aback. Her little house wasn't ostentatious or fancy. It was small, simple. It actually reminded him a great deal of *his* house. "Nice place."

Sophie's smile proved she was quite fond of her home. "It's a rental, not mine, but I love it. The neighborhood's quiet and safe and the rent is affordable. I've been here for nearly two years."

Marc got out of the car, intending to open Sophie's door

for her. She beat him to it, stepping out. As he rounded the hood, he caught her wince. "Are you okay?"

She nodded, though she was still grimacing. "My feet are killing me."

He glanced down at her high heels. "No wonder."

She gave him an annoyed look. "I'm usually fine in my heels, but I was on my feet more than I'd expected tonight. Plus these shoes are new and not exactly broken in."

He offered his arm, which she took with unexpected ease, leaning on it enough to let him know she wasn't kidding about her aching feet. When they reached the front porch, she opened the door then turned to smile at him.

"Thanks for the ride home."

He glanced through the open doorway. She'd left a light on in the living room, allowing him to see part of her couch. "Come on."

She frowned. "Excuse me."

He didn't reply, just grasped her hand and led her to the couch. He gestured for her to sit down. "Take off your shoes."

Sophie's hands flew to her hips as her scowl grew. She clearly didn't like being told what to do. He didn't give her a chance to yell at him for his domineering attitude. Instead, he grabbed her by the waist, pulling her toward him for a quick kiss.

It had the desired effect. She was stunned speechless long enough for him to get his way. He guided her down onto the couch and pulled off her shoes.

She started to stand, her face flushed, though he wasn't sure if it was anger or lust supplying the color. "How dare you—"

He lifted her legs and claimed the cushion beneath them, placing her feet on his lap. His relentless grip prevented her from rising. "Hush. I happen to give the world's best foot massages." To prove his point, he applied pressure to the sole of one of her feet.

Sophie groaned and fell back against a throw pillow. He repeated the motion on her other foot. "Holy shit," she muttered. "That feels so good."

He tried to ignore her almost seductive purr, but it was too late. His cock responded to her soft moans and slow stretches as he continued rubbing her feet. He imagined this was how she'd look if he lifted her skirt and offered her a different kind of massage.

If he touched her pussy right now, how wet would she be?

His hard-on grew larger, the damn thing throbbing almost painfully. Much as he wanted to pretend otherwise, tonight wasn't going to end with sex, no matter how much his cock may protest. There was still too much distrust floating between them.

He kept working, applying equal measures of deep rubs and soft strokes. Twice her feet brushed against the front placket of his slacks. He wondered if she could feel his erection.

When she rubbed against it once more and lingered, his gaze flew to her face. She was watching him—and she knew *exactly* what she was touching.

She pressed her toes more firmly against his cock, giving her own version of a foot massage. Marc swallowed heavily and tried to ignore how fucking good her playful toes felt. But soon he reached a point of no return. He grasped

Sophie's ankle, halting her movements. "I need to leave now, Soph, or I won't leave at all."

She lay still. He could practically see the wheels spinning in her brain. She wanted to invite him to stay as much as she wanted him to leave.

Fair enough. It was too soon. He offered her a wry grin. They didn't know each other well enough. Yet. He'd correct that problem. Sophie was about to start seeing a hell of a lot more of him.

He lifted her legs off his lap and rose. Sophie started to sit up, but he placed his hand on her shoulder and pushed her back against the cushions. Leaning over, he placed a soft kiss to her forehead.

"I'll see you tomorrow."

Sophie sighed softly then accepted his departure with good humor. "Thanks for the warning...and the foot massage. Good night, Marc."

"Night, princess."

CHAPTER THREE

Sophie sat in the living room of the house she'd grown up in and marveled over how foreign the place seemed to her these days. The house felt less like a home than the rental she lived in. Since her mother's death, the place had gotten...colder. Her father employed a full-time housekeeper who kept the place so spotless it looked as if no one lived there at all. Recently Dad had also hired an interior decorator who'd taken out her mother's comfortable, airy décor and replaced it with the stark, leathery bachelor's pad she was now sitting in.

When she'd arrived, the housekeeper had led her to this room to wait for her dad, who was on a business call in his office. It was her own family's home, and yet she'd been ushered in like a stranger. She briefly wondered if the woman was standing guard outside the closed door, ready to attack should Sophie attempt to break out.

Rising from the couch, she walked to the mantel, looking at the old pictures that were the only holdout from the days when she and her mother had lived here. There were a couple large, professionally done family portraits of her and her parents. One from when she was only a toddler and another showing her in that horribly awkward middle-school stage. Of all the things her father had thrown out, she was sorry that crappy picture hadn't been part of the trash.

Sophie's gaze only touched on the portraits. It was the two smaller informal pictures her mother had framed herself that she preferred.

In one, a very young version of her parents sat side by side in a restaurant, looking at each other and laughing. It was taken before she was born, but it reminded her that her parents had been genuinely in love. Not that she really doubted that. It was simply a trick of time. The more of it that passed and the colder her father became, the less she was able to remember him as the handsome, carefree man who would have moved Heaven and Earth for his beautiful wife.

The second picture was of Sophie and her dad the day her parents brought her home from the hospital. He was cradling her in his arms as if she was the most precious thing he'd ever held. Her mother hadn't been the only woman to receive her father's adoration. At that moment in time, Dad had thought she'd hung the moon too.

She sniffled, trying to batten down the strange sadness that had crept over her.

"Sophia." Her father's deep voice rumbled behind her, and she was surprised to realize how close he was. She hadn't even heard him come in.

She blinked quickly in an attempt to hide her tears, then pasted on a fake smile and turned to face him.

Jasper Kennedy was still a handsome man, though now his looks fell more in the distinguished category, rather than the hottie column where Marc resided.

Shit. Why on earth was she thinking about Marc *now?*

She knew why. He was the reason she was here.

"How are you, darling?" her father asked, stepping forward to offer an awkward peck on the cheek.

When had they stopped hugging? When had they become mere acquaintances? Her stomach ached for the days when she could curl up on her daddy's lap and he'd tell her stories about the places he'd visited, always promising that when she was older, he'd take her with him. The ten-year-old still lurking inside wanted to ask if he'd brought her a souvenir back from his last business trip.

She was becoming maudlin. *Grow up, Soph.*

"I'm fine. How was your trip to Greece?"

Her father gestured to the couch. She resumed her seat as he claimed the oversized leather recliner across from her. "It was very productive."

"Did you get to see any of the sights? Play tourist?"

Dad grinned, shaking his head. "No time, I'm afraid."

His answer made her feel even sadder. More than fifteen years had passed since her mother's death, and while Sophie had tried her best to carry on, it occurred to her that her father had moved forward in a way that was less about living and more about existing.

Dad looked at his watch covertly. She was throwing off his routine. Ordinarily that gesture would annoy her, but today she was too melancholy. It was as if her eyes had been opened to some pretty hard truths, and she didn't like facing them.

"I've been hearing some rumors."

Dad, rather absentmindedly, said, "Oh?"

Sophie had spent the past several years getting used to having only half his attention. She wasn't going to accept it this time. "How could you try to close down the community center? Portland needs that place."

Her father sighed, and she got the sense he wasn't surprised by what had brought her here. He knew how much she loved the center. What it had meant to her mother. He must have known she would react this way. And yet, he still pursued the purchase.

"I think it's outgrown its usefulness at this point."

"Bullshit."

"Sophia," he chastised.

He never called her Sophie or Soph anymore. When she'd taken over his party-hostess duties, he'd opted for the formal version of her name. "Sophia" certainly sounded more sophisticated and projected the snooty, detached air her father seemed hell-bent on maintaining. She hadn't protested the change, though now she wondered if she should have. She hated the way *Sophia* sounded coming from his lips.

"Dad, that place offers so many amazing programs. How can you say it's not useful?"

"There are a lot of things you don't know. The building is in desperate need of repairs. It's not safe."

Her temper sparked. "It was perfectly safe until the building inspector decided to nitpick over a lot of insignificant problems. A leaky sink is a danger? Really?" During his visit to Books and Brew yesterday, Marc had shown her the list of so-called "problems" with the building's structure. It was obvious the inspector had been encouraged to find problems where none truly existed. Even after a second walk-through—at the request of the community center—the second inspector backed up the first, listing even more insignificant items to be repaired.

Her father's brow creased. "Who have you been talking to?"

Shit. "No one."

Her father wasn't appeased by the answer, but he let it go. "There are other issues besides the facility itself. The board of trustees has made some questionable decisions regarding the use of funds and—"

"And they were audited and cleared."

Again, Dad fell silent. "You've been doing your homework." For a moment, she thought she detected a small bit of pride in his voice.

"You know what that place means to me. Mom used to take me there for dance lessons when I was little. The summer camps and family picnics were a huge part of my childhood. Why would you try to deprive other children of those experiences?"

Dad rose and walked to the mantel. "How many times have I told you, Sophia? It's not personal, it's business."

She sucked in a deep, furious breath. That fucking line had become his mantra since her mother had died. She hated it. "No. Not this time. This time it *is* personal."

"The trustees have two months to raise the funds to save the center. After that, I *will* buy the property."

"To build another shopping mall that the city doesn't need."

Dad smiled, but his eyes betrayed no happiness. "Consider this—the money made at that mall will add to your inheritance."

The words felt like a slap to the face. "I don't want your fucking money!"

Dad scowled. "Sophia. *Everything* I do, I do for you."

She shook her head. "No. Don't heap that crap at my feet. Everything you do, you do for *yourself*. But not this time. Thanks to you, I've had years of practice organizing fundraisers for worthy causes. You're about to reap what you've sown."

With that, she headed for the door. For a moment, she thought she heard her father call her back, his gentle voice reminding her of the way it used to sound, but she dismissed it as wishful thinking.

She knew what she had to do, even though the thought of going to war with her dad brought her no joy. In fact, she felt as if she'd been punched in the stomach. Hard.

This wasn't going to be easy...and she'd need help.

A BELL JINGLED in the lobby but Marc didn't look up. He was knee-deep in paperwork, trying to find some loophole that could buy the community center more time. Then he faced a long afternoon of preparing a witness for a murder trial that was scheduled to start tomorrow. When it rained, it poured.

He rubbed his forehead, trying to fend off the tension headache building behind his eyes.

"Rough day?"

He glanced up at the sound of Sophie's voice, pleased to see her.

"I've had better." It had started far too early, after a restless night spent tossing and turning and jacking off while fantasizing about the society princess currently leaning against his doorjamb.

He'd been disappointed when Sophie had called him a couple of days earlier to say Jared had helped her jumpstart her car. To make up for the missed opportunity to see her, he'd stopped by Books and Brew last night for a beer. As usual, the conversation had ended up in a disagreement about her father and, like a jackass, he'd shared too many details about the community center case in a self-serving need to prove he was right. His father *had* always told him pride would be his downfall.

What dear old Dad failed to realize was that when his pride joined forces with his cock, he became the biggest fool on Earth.

Worst part was, even now, he didn't regret the things he'd told Sophie. His instincts screamed that he could trust her.

"Yeah. My day has pretty much sucked too." Sophie walked in and claimed one of the two chairs across from his desk. She glanced around the room. "Your office is ridiculously small."

"Thanks for pointing out the obvious." She was right. Every available inch of space was filled with papers, files, law books. "Free legal aid doesn't pay much."

She laughed. "Does it pay anything?"

"A little bit."

"Not to sound rude, but what made you choose this

career path? I mean, I think this is awesome and all, but it seems to me you could be making bank anywhere else."

He didn't take offense at her question. God knew it was one he'd been asked a million times in the past few years. "I did the big law firm deal right after graduation. I was on the fast track to a partnership."

"Sounds profitable."

"It was. Very."

"So why would you give that up for this glamorous inside office with no view?" she asked.

"I was twenty-nine with high blood pressure and suffering from my third ulcer in as many years. I didn't date, ate all my meals at my desk and slept less than five hours a night, usually on the couch in my office. At my yearly checkup, my doctor informed me I was a prime candidate for a heart attack."

"Ouch."

"I walked out of his office and realized I was sick of it all. I turned in my resignation and walked away. Decided I'd use my powers for good rather than money."

Sophie fell silent for a moment. He wondered if she was appalled by his decision.

Sophie glanced around his office once more. "That's pretty gutsy, Marc. And very, very cool."

Her words were completely sincere, and once again he was struck by how different the real Sophie was from the one he had created in his mind. "My parents' response was the opposite of yours. You say 'gutsy', they say 'insane'. You say 'cool', they say 'What the hell are you thinking?'."

Her brow creased, and for the first time, he noticed sadness in her eyes. "I guess it's obvious you went against their advice. Are they okay with your decision now? Are you still close to your parents?"

He leaned back in his chair. "I'm not going to lie. We had a rough year or two. Lots of family holidays have ended in arguments, but they're getting there. Enough time has passed that they know my decision wasn't just a whim. That I'm serious about what I want to do with my life. The main problem was, it was my dad's law firm that I quit."

"Jesus."

Marc chuckled. "Yeah. Well. Dad suffered a minor heart attack last year and I think it's opened his eyes to why I made the decision I did. Since then, I've noticed the disappointed looks he used to heap on me have disappeared. He's started asking about my work here when before he pretended I didn't have a job at all."

"That's progress then. It's a shame it took something like a heart attack for him to realize the work you do here is good. And important."

Her words touched him more than he could say. If anyone would understand how he'd grown up, the pressure that had been put on him to succeed, to make money at any cost, it was probably Sophie.

He'd given up his former life while fighting to keep his identity relatively anonymous in Portland. He was deter-mined to keep all of that in the past, but something about Sophie made him long to share confidences.

Marc pushed the thought away. He'd already stepped over the line last night, telling her things he shouldn't have. Time to put some space between them. "I don't think you came here today to hear my life story. What's up?"

Sophie bent forward, resting her elbows on her knees. "I want to hold a fundraiser for the community center."

Marc blew out a long breath. "Soph. I know you don't think your dad is involved in purchasing the property, but—"

"I know he's trying to close down the center."

For a week, Sophie had stood her ground, insisting her father would never be involved in the shady dealings surrounding the community center while trying to get in touch with her old man. Looked as if she'd succeeded. "You do?"

"He's back in town. I went to see him this morning. He told me he was trying to buy the property and what he hoped to do with it. I basically told him I'd stop him."

Marc didn't respond immediately as he tried to picture Sophie and Jasper going at it head-to-head. In the past, he would have put his money on Jasper, but after spending time in Sophie's presence, he had no doubt she could hold her own in an argument with her dad.

"We have less than two months, Soph. The kind of fundraising we'd need to arrange would have to be on a large scale. Events like that take longer than a few weeks to organize."

"I know, but I've already got something in the works. Originally, the dinner last night was phase one in a two-part charity drive for the domestic abuse shelter. I stopped by there to talk to Jenna, the manager of the shelter, before I came here. The second fundraiser, a bachelor auction, is set to take place in a few weeks. Jenna agrees that the center needs to be saved. So many of the women and children who seek shelter at her place have benefited from the programs offered at the center. We've decided all the money taken in at the bachelor auction will be used to help with the improvements needed at the center."

For the first time in days, Marc felt a spark of hope. Even so, he couldn't sugarcoat things for Sophie. "The funds needed are fairly substantial. I'm not sure one fundraiser will do it."

"Maybe not, but I called Casey Woods on my way here. Do you know Casey?"

Marc nodded. "Only by reputation. He did all the renovations on the Crawford Inn, where your benefit dinner took place, right?"

"Yeah, that's him. He's done some work at Books and Brew over the past year or so—and he's also got the hots for Jordan. I told him about the center and he's offered his services in making the repairs. He'll work at cost."

Marc reared back. "No way! You're kidding me?"

Sophie shook her head. "I also have a call in to Gabriel Lawson. We rent the space for Books and Brew from him and he's become a good friend. I'm hoping I can convince him to match whatever we raise at the auction."

"You think he would?"

Sophie wiggled her eyebrows. "Let's just say I think Jordan could help me persuade him to. After I leave here, I'm going to visit Patricia Butt–Bi— Er, Butler–Baines."

Marc feigned a shudder. "Why in the hell would you want to see that woman?"

"Because as annoying as she is, she's also extremely useful in certain circles. She owes me a favor and she's going to pay up."

"How?"

"She's going to help me strong-arm every attractive,

eligible man in the city into participating, and then she's going to make sure all her rich, man-hungry girlfriends are there to place bids."

Marc stood up and walked around his desk. He took her hands and pulled her to her feet. "You're incredible."

She grinned. "There has to be some perks to being a society princess."

Marc couldn't resist. He kissed her.

Sophie accepted his embrace as easily as she had in the coat closet. Marc sensed there was something more brewing beneath the surface. He broke the kiss, though he didn't move away.

"Are you okay, Soph?"

Sophie's grip on his shoulders tightened as she pressed her body closer. "I'm not sure. My dad—" She paused before shaking her head. "I don't want to think about him right now. I just need..." Again her words faded way. Her breasts brushed against his chest. He knew exactly what she needed. Distraction and comfort.

Unfortunately, Marc was far too aware of the fact his receptionist, Janice, was sitting just outside that open door. He gently pushed her away.

"Don't move," he murmured. Walking to the lobby, he told Janice she could head out for lunch early. The receptionist jumped at the chance for a long break. Marc followed her to the front door, flipped the sign from open to closed then locked it.

Sophie watched him from the doorway.

"I thought I told you not to move."

"You're closing?"

He nodded.

"Pretty sure of yourself, aren't you?"

He chuckled as he approached, slowly backing her into his office until he could shut that door as well. He flipped the lock. "Yep. I am."

"Good."

He continued to move until the backs of her legs touched his desk. He cleared the papers on top to one side then lifted her to the surface. "Have I ever told you how much I like the short skirts you wear?"

She reached for his tie. "No, but that's hardly surprising considering we've only known each other about a week and a half."

Her comment, though funny, also seemed wrong. "It feels like longer than that."

She bit her lower lip. "I know. It's weird, isn't it?"

They'd been thrown together by a common cause and circumstances. Marc had never felt so grateful for dumb luck. Still, he couldn't let go of the worry tugging at the edge of his conscience. "What's your dad going to say when he finds out about the fundraiser? It could wreck his business deal."

Sophie lifted her shoulders in the universal "I don't know" gesture. "It won't be a shock. I told him I was going to wreck it."

He tucked a loose strand of long blonde hair behind her ear. "He's still family."

"My dad and I haven't exactly been close the past two, three, fifteen years or so." He knew she meant her words as a joke, but there was a deep-seated sorrow in her eyes that killed the humor.

Marc ran his fingers through her soft hair. It fell in sexy

waves over her shoulders. "I don't think what you're doing is going to mend any fences."

Her face was sad. Marc was sorry he'd brought up the subject, but there'd been something in her expression when he'd talked about his own relationship with his parents that told him she wasn't exactly comfortable with what she was doing. Despite their estrangement, Sophie clearly loved her dad very much.

Sophie loosened his tie. "Do you mind if we talk about something else? Or maybe we could talk about nothing at all."

Marc cupped her cheeks, cradling her face as he bent to kiss her again. He was okay with silence. Sophie moaned softly when his hands drifted down to gently stroke her breasts through her blouse. Well, maybe not complete silence. He liked her quiet sexy noises whenever he kissed or touched her. She never left him guessing about what she liked.

The sound of silk on cotton filled the room as Sophie dragged his tie away from the collar of his shirt. Her fingers began working to free the buttons. Marc briefly considered how stupid he'd been to start something so heated here, during working hours. While there was nothing he wanted more than to fuck Sophie into oblivion, he preferred the idea of taking her for the first time in the comfort of his own bed, when they had all the time in the world. Right now, the clock was ticking on Janice's lunch break and the rest of his work-day. His schedule was ridiculously tight.

Sophie was a fast worker. She slipped his shirt from his shoulders, letting it fall to the floor. Her fingers explored his bare chest, toying with the light smattering of hair there.

Marc marveled at how quickly she was relieving him of his clothing. He gently grasped her wrists when she reached for the buckle on his belt.

She tried to shake him off, but he tightened his grip. "Slow down."

Sophie shook her head. "No. I don't want to. Last night, after you left the bar..."

She'd obviously spent the night suffering from unrequited lust too. He could appreciate the feeling.

The phone in the reception area rang. Again, he cursed his impulsiveness.

"We're going to have sex, Sophie. Make no mistake about that. It's just not going to happen here, today."

She glanced at his face, frustration radiating from her. "Why not? You've locked the door. There's no one here."

"Because that phone's going to keep ringing. My receptionist is going to come back. I have someone stopping by for a meeting in..." He lifted his arm to look at his watch. "Shit. In thirty minutes."

She frowned. "Then why did you start this?"

It was his turn to shrug. "I have no idea. You come around and I stop thinking with the right head."

She laughed. "Yeah. I get that. I'm not usually quite so..." She paused, searching for a word.

"Horny?"

She rolled her eyes. "I was thinking 'easy', but horny works too. I haven't had sex in a while."

"That's right. Probably hard to find someone after Chuck."

"Ugh. You know, it's bad form to keep bringing up that asshole."

Marc placed a soft kiss on the tip of her nose. "Agreed. So was he your last boyfriend?"

"Boyfriend, yes. Sex, no."

Marc tried to keep his face impassive, but he must've failed, letting his surprise peek through.

"Jesus, Marc. You do realize I'm not *really* a princess, don't you? I'm not always searching for Prince Charming or romance. Sometimes I just like to have sex."

He grinned and decided on the spot that Sophia Kennedy was the hottest woman he'd ever met. He was about as romantic as a bull in heat, and no girlfriend in the past had ever accused him of being too charming. "Just sex" was *just fine* with him, but that didn't solve their current problem of time.

Sophie wasn't helping things either. Her hand returned to the front placket of his slacks, and she lightly caressed the bulge he didn't bother to hide. If she kept that up, he'd say to hell with everything and take her anyway.

He caught sight of the tie she'd stripped off him. A dirty plan formed in his mind. Maybe they didn't have time for sex, but they sure as hell had time to do a little messing around.

Grasping the necktie, he pulled her hands behind her back. Sophie jerked with astonishment as he knotted the tie around her wrists, quickly and efficiently.

"Hey."

He pressed a hard kiss on her lips to silence her. He could feel her struggling to escape the bonds. Lifting a hand, he loosely touched her throat, feeling for her pulse. It was definitely elevated but not alarmingly so. She wasn't afraid.

He stood up straighter and studied her face. "Are you okay?"

Her brow creased. "You didn't seriously just tie me up, did you?"

"Yep. You like it?"

She fought against the knot, but he was no stranger to bondage. It would hold until he released her. "Untie me."

"Nope."

"Marc."

"Is the tie cutting off circulation?"

She shook her head.

"Is it hurting you?"

Again, she shook her head.

"Then I'm leaving it on. Just for a minute. I like the idea of having you at my mercy." As he spoke, he began to unbutton her blouse. Sophie's chest rose and fell faster as her breathing increased. Again, he studied her face. "I'm not going to hurt you, Soph. I'd never hurt you. You know that, right?"

"We've only known each other a couple weeks."

He wondered if she kept repeating that fact to remind herself. He was having a hard time holding on to it too. "I know. Trust me anyway," he whispered.

Once her shirt was unbuttoned, he pushed it over her shoulders. The material tangled with the tie at her wrists. He left it there.

She licked her lips, her gaze never leaving his.

"Beautiful," he murmured as he placed a soft kiss on her cheek. He pushed the straps of her bra off her shoulders. Instead of unfastening the lacy concoction, he reached inside the cups and lifted her breasts out. With her arms behind her and her breasts resting on top of the bra, she made a gorgeous display.

He bent forward to suck first one then the other nipple into his mouth. He teased the tight nubs with his tongue as Sophie began to squirm on the desk. Her legs were pressed tightly together, and he imagined she was trying to find some sort of relief from the building pressure.

He nipped the tip he was currently playing with just enough to make her squeal, then moan. There was a fine line between pleasure and pain. It appeared Sophie wasn't opposed to crossing it. He cataloged that idea for future reference.

Taking a step back, he surveyed his work. Sophie was disheveled and sexy, pin-up-model worthy. He committed the way she looked to memory, knowing he'd never seen any woman look more stunning.

Sophie was flushed from his attention to her breasts, her nipples hard and rosy-red. His mouth watered for another taste—but there was something else he wanted more.

He placed his hands on her waist. "Stand up for a second."

She scooted off the desk with more grace than he would have thought possible considering her bound hands.

When she stood before him, he reached for the hem of her short skirt and slowly lifted the silky fabric until it cleared her hips. "Sit back down."

Sophie reclaimed her seat on the edge of the desk. Marc reached beneath her knees and slowly spread her legs apart.

"Christ. A thong," he whispered.

Even bound, Sophie was far from an inactive participant in their play. She stretched out her legs and wrapped her ankles around his hips in an effort to draw him nearer. "I'm starting to feel like a *Playboy* model, the way you keep posing me."

He allowed her to pull him closer. She had on a different pair of strappy heels. He briefly wondered how many pairs of sexy shoes he'd find in her closet. Then he pictured himself using the shoe straps to bind her spread-eagle to his bed. "What can I say? You're inspiring all sorts of kinky thoughts in my head."

"Like what?" Her question fell out on a breathless sigh.

"There are a million things I want to do with you. Tie you to my bed. Blindfold you. Gag you. Use dildos, butt plugs, nipple clamps on you. I'll take you from behind, upside down, sideways. I want to fuck you in a pool, a car, on a mountainside, at a football game."

She laughed. "I hate football."

"We wouldn't be watching the game. So what do you think? Feel like spending a few weeks—or months—exploring your naughty side with me?"

"I think I lied. You might be out of *my* league. I'm afraid the kinkiest I've ever gotten is sex in the alley behind Books and Brew and a little bit of anal play. Not at the same time," she quickly added.

Marc's smile grew. She was too perfect—funny, honest, straightforward. "Take some time to think about it. You can give me what I want later."

"Are you always so sure of yourself?"

Marc winked. "Let's just say I'm very good at reading people."

Her face betrayed exactly how much she wanted to knock him down a peg for being so cocky. He also knew she wouldn't because despite her desire to one-up him for his arrogance, deep down inside, Sophie was dying to be a bad girl.

"This is one case you're going to lose," she said, her trembling voice in direct opposition to the strong words.

"We'll see." He knelt before her, loving the sound of her quick, excited intake of breath.

"Marc..." she started.

"Shh. I'm gathering evidence."

She lifted one leg, her ankle coming around his shoulder, touching him in a way that let him know she was completely into this game. "What?"

"I'm looking for proof that everything I said turns you on so much, there's no way you'll say no to my offer of nonstop kinky sex."

She opened her mouth to reply, but he quickly cut off any clever retort by running his finger along the thin—and soaking wet—string of her thong.

"Aha," he said softly. He glanced up and captured her gaze. "You're not as innocent as you claim."

She closed her eyes when he moved the thin strip of material to one side, leaving her pussy open to his questing fingers. "Do you always talk this much?"

He chuckled. "Curse of a lawyer. Most of us are way too fond of the sound of our own voices."

"Marc?"

"Yeah?"

"Shut up." She wrapped her other ankle around his shoulder and nudged him closer, telling him without words exactly what kind of lip action she was interested in.

"My pleasure," he said—then pressed his lips to her pussy.

Sophie reacted like a sprinter to the starter pistol, her hips jerking when he opened his mouth and sucked deeply on her clit.

"Oh my God." Sophie's head flew back as he used his teeth, lips and tongue to drive her arousal higher. She obviously hadn't been kidding about her dry spell. She was primed and ready to roll. He suspected it wouldn't take much to drive her to climax. Ordinarily he liked to drag out the foreplay, build the anticipation, but their time was already running out. As it was, he was facing a long, painful afternoon, working with the mother of all erections.

Marc increased the suction on her clit, and Sophie gasped.

"So freaking good."

He added his fingers to the play, sliding one, then two inside her pussy. Sophie's hips thrust forward, seeking more, silently prodding him to go deeper and faster.

He complied, placing his lips back on her clit and sucking hard.

Sophie fell apart, her body trembling as her orgasm took over. Her legs tightened, trapping his head. He smiled at her strength and figured there were worse places to be ensnared than between Sophie's thighs.

When she began to calm down, he lightly lifted her legs from his shoulders and stood. Reaching around her, he unbound her hands.

Sophie moved like lightning, catching him off guard.

She had his belt unbuckled and his pants undone and around his ankles before he could gather his wits enough to respond. She claimed the spot he'd just vacated, kneeling before him.

His hands flew to her hair. "Soph, wait. There's no time."

She didn't respond. Instead, she ran her tongue along his hard cock from root to tip.

Fuck it. His client could wait.

His fingers tightened in her long tresses as she took the head of his dick inside her hot mouth.

Jesus. She didn't hold anything back, didn't act coy, didn't hesitate. She took him deeper before sucking, her cheeks hollowing around his flesh. The action sent shards of electricity through him and his balls grew heavy. It was going too fast, but he'd be damned if he'd slow things down. Sophie was sucking on his cock like it was a lollipop, humming, licking, teasing with her teeth.

When she wrapped her hand around the base of his cock, squeezing so tightly he saw stars, he knew it was pointless to resist.

"God, Soph. I can't stop. If you don't want—"

She increased her speed and suction, and Marc lost it. Hot spurts of come flew from the tip of his dick, and Sophie drank down every last drop.

"Mother of God." Marc dropped to his knees in front of her, grasping her head and pulling her close for another kiss. No force of nature could have kept him away from her at that moment.

Sophie, as always, returned the embrace...with interest. She was passionate, sexy and fucking hot as hell.

Marc was suddenly starting to suspect he'd met the woman of his dreams, fresh from the society pages.

Fate was laughing its ass off right now.

CHAPTER FOUR

"Hey, grumpy ass. What gives?"

Sophie scowled at Stephanie as she placed dirty glasses on the bar. "Nothing."

Stephanie poured a beer from the tap, looking as annoyed as Sophie felt. "Don't say 'nothing'. You've been walking around here like a bitch from hell for well over two weeks. I'm PMSing and in no mood to watch you slamming drinks around for another night."

Sophie wanted to be angry, but Steph's assessment was spot-on. She'd been a bear for weeks. She sank onto one of the barstools and sighed. "I fucked up."

Jayne, who'd been setting up a new window display of books, came over and took the stool next to her. Eavesdropping was the number one form of entertainment on slow days at the store. "Fucked up how?"

"With Marc."

"Marc Garrett?" Stephanie asked.

Sophie nodded. She hadn't said much to her friends

about the attorney who'd been twisting her in knots for weeks. For one, there wasn't much *to* say. She hadn't laid eyes on the man since their little tête-à-tête in his office nearly three weeks earlier.

"Wait a second. I need to do something." Stephanie grabbed her phone and began texting.

"What?" Sophie asked.

"I'm telling Jordan to get her ass down here. We've all been worried about you, but we didn't know what was bugging you. Sounds like we're about to get the goods."

Sophie tried to be annoyed, but she couldn't summon the emotion. Obviously it had done no good, telling herself to forget Marc. Maybe it was time to call in the recruits and ask for help. She glanced around the bar. Apart from a couple of young guys chilling out with beers at a table near the front and a woman perusing the magazines in the corner of the bookstore, there was no one else in the place to bother them.

Jordan appeared at the bottom of the stairs in record time. "Thank God you're finally talking. I've been worried sick about you."

Sophie smirked, unable to resist teasing her friend. "If you've had time to think about *me*, then clearly Gabe and Casey suck in the sack. Maybe you need to reconsider this threesome setup."

Jordan flushed. "Don't worry about my guys. They do just fine in bed."

Stephanie laughed. "God. That deal is going to take some getting used to. When our Jordan decides to jump back into the dating scene, she fucking dives in headfirst."

Jordan bit her lip and asked the same question she had

almost daily since she, Casey and Gabriel had entered a ménage affair. "You guys are sure this is okay? I mean—"

"It's fine!" Jayne, Stephanie and Sophie repeated in unison.

Jayne grasped Jordan's hand. "You're still happy, right?"

Jordan nodded.

"Then that's all that matters." Jayne's philosophy on life. No matter what the world threw at them, Jayne's main concern was always that they walk the path that would lead them to happiness.

It was a good idea...in theory. In reality, Sophie was struggling to figure out what might make her happy. In her career, her family issues and her relationships, she never seemed able to grasp that elusive happiness. It was frustrating as hell.

"Well, we're not here to talk about me, are we? What's going on, Soph? You're always so upbeat and energetic. It's not like you to be down for so long."

Stephanie placed a Heineken in front of her. "She said she fucked up with Marc Garrett."

"The attorney?" Jordan asked.

Sophie was grateful for the liquid courage. She took a long drink of the ice-cold beer. "Yeah. We were hanging out quite a bit a few weeks ago and I sort of thought things were heading in a good direction, but now I'm thinking I threw us off course."

"Is there a reason why you're speaking in generalizations? I thought you hated the guy. You called him an asshole...repeatedly. Stop screwing around and give us specific details." Stephanie poured herself half a beer from the tap.

Sophie groaned. Stephanie was the queen of no-nonsense. "I lied about the asshole part. Truth is I really like him. A lot."

Jayne pulled a bowl of peanuts closer and began cracking the shell on one. "Did I miss something? You two have never even gone out on a date, have you?"

Sophie picked at the label on her beer. "No. No dates. I mean, we talked when he came by here that one night. We sat next to each other at Patricia Butt–Bitch's party and had a good time. Then we sort of made out in the coat closet at the Crawford Inn."

"I knew it!" Jordan piped in. "I knew something had happened that night, but I couldn't figure out what."

"He cornered me."

"Good kisser?" Stephanie asked.

"An amazing kisser. My car battery died that night, so Marc drove me home."

Stephanie leaned closer and rubbed her hands together. "Something tells me we're getting to the good part."

Sophie shook her head. "Sorry to disappoint you, but he just gave me a foot massage and left that night. It was actually a few days later, in his office, when things got hot and heavy."

Stephanie put down the beer she'd just lifted. "*How* hot and how heavy? Spare no expense in the description."

Sophie laughed. She loved her friends. They always listened, never judged. She'd been an idiot to try to deal with her anxiety alone these past few weeks. "We made out."

Stephanie made a sound like a buzzer. "Errr! Lame answer. Try again."

Sophie rolled her eyes. "Fine. He went down on me and I gave him a blowjob. Detailed enough for you?"

"Better. So that was what? Two, three weeks ago?" Stephanie asked.

Now they were getting to the heart of the matter. "Almost three. And yeah. Since then...nothing."

Jayne, the most compassionate of the group, reached over and took Sophie's hand. "What happened?"

Sophie shrugged. "I have no idea. I've called him a few times but whenever I suggest we get together, he always has an excuse why he can't."

Jordan frowned. "What sort of excuses?"

"Apparently he's defending a man who's been accused of murder. The trial's going on a lot longer than he'd anticipated. Then last weekend he had to make a quick trip back home to DC for some family emergency, and he's also working to find a loophole that may buy the community center more time to raise the funds needed for repairs."

Jordan's face cleared. "Those sound like pretty good reasons to me. He's just been busy."

"I know, Jordan. They're all valid, even noble reasons." Sophie tried to tell herself she was being a petty, selfish bitch, but she couldn't shake the idea that karma was teaching her a lesson. How many times in the past had she played the "I'm too busy" card as a way to avoid an interested suitor? Hell, she was a master at the game. "Do you think I made a mistake with the blowjob? We'd only known each other a week or so. I'm afraid maybe I came off as slutty."

Stephanie slapped her hand against the bar. "Holy shit. Really, Soph? That's what you think went wrong? I thought you said he went down on you too."

"He did."

"Fine. Then if you're a slut, so is he. Goddamn double standards piss me off. I highly doubt that's why he's not calling you, but if it is, then you're better off without the judgmental prick."

Sophie felt her face flushing despite the fact she should be used to Stephanie's brutal honesty. Plus, hearing her friend's assertions made her realize how stupid her concern was. "I actually don't really think that's why he's avoiding me."

Jordan grinned. "If he's a straight guy, I'm one hundred percent sure that's not the problem. I don't know any man who dumps a girl for giving him a blowjob."

They all laughed, but Sophie was forced to admit she'd been building mountains out of molehills, spending the last few weeks grasping at any excuse simply to avoid admitting the truth.

"I think it all boils down to the fact he's just not interested in me. I should've seen it when he volunteered to be auctioned off."

Jayne squeezed her hand gently. "Then it's his loss."

She nodded, wishing there weren't tears forming in her eyes. "Yeah. Problem is, I really liked him. I thought we clicked. It's stupid to let this get me down. We never even went out on a date. It's just..." Her words faded away.

Stephanie was first to break the silence. "I knew Jared was the guy for me the first night we met. It took me a while to admit it, but I get what you're saying. You can tell when you connect with someone pretty early in the game."

Jordan stepped closer and put her hand on Sophie's shoulder. "I understand that feeling too. While Gabe and I have been friends forever, Casey and I are just at the beginning of our relationship. Even so, I feel like I've known him for years."

Sophie smiled and swiped away the tears. They really did understand. "So what do I do now?"

Jayne released her hand and stood up. "You take it a day at a time. Luckily the next few days are going to be too busy for you to be sad. It's T-minus seven days and counting on this big bachelor auction, and we've got a gazillion things to do between now and then to get this place ready."

Jayne was right. Sophie had been working on a to-do list earlier this morning. After listing twenty time-consuming tasks that needed to happen to make the auction a success, she'd stopped adding to the list. In her current down-in-the-dumps state of mind, it had all seemed too daunting and overwhelming. Now it was the answer to a prayer. Keeping busy was just the trick to setting aside her sadness over Marc's disinterest.

"Good plan. I'll start with the stage setup. My cousin is letting me borrow a makeshift one he uses for his garage band. It has spotlights and everything. He's also loaning me sound equipment. He sent me specs and it should all fit in here fine. We'll just have to clear out the tables on that side of the bar." Sophie pointed to her right.

The original plan had always been to hold the auction at Books and Brew. Sophie had thought it would be good PR for the store, and the initial intent was for a more intimate event. However, now that the charity had changed and the need to make lots of money for the center was hanging over Sophie's head, she regretted offering up the smaller space.

Unfortunately there wasn't time to find a larger venue, given the short time frame.

Her friends—God bless them—had agreed they'd clear out as much space as needed, vowing they'd make the auction a success.

"Is this the cousin who lives in Seattle?" Jayne asked.

Sophie nodded. "Yep. I'm taking a little road trip tomorrow. Borrowing Casey's truck to pick up all the stuff. I'll be gone most of the day. Actually, between now and the auction, I'm not sure how much help I'll be around the bar."

Stephanie threw her a quick wave of the hand. "We can cover for you. We're closing the day before and of the auction anyway to set stuff up. If the cleanup looks too daunting, we'll close the day after too, so don't worry about it. We're good to go on this."

Jordan agreed. "Yep. No problem. I've been meaning to tell you how great I think it is that you're working so hard to save the community center. I love that place. It would be hard to picture this city without it."

"I think you're brave to stand up to your dad," Jayne chimed in.

"Brave nothing," Stephanie said with a big grin. "Our social butterfly is turning into queen of the ball-busters. I have to admit I prefer this new you."

"Yeah right. Well, don't be too impressed. Inside, I'm a nervous wreck. What if we don't make enough money?"

Jordan glanced over when one of the two male customers waved for their attention. "You will. Gabe was talking about it last night. He said if anyone could do it, you could." Jordan walked over to grab the men's empty glasses and nodded when they asked for another round.

Sophie took a deep breath and smiled.

Positive thinking. That was all she needed. A little positive thinking.

The auction would be a success.

They'd raise the needed money for the center.

She'd show her father that personal is always better than business.

And she'd forget all about Marc Garrett.

Hopefully.

THE NIGHT of the auction arrived far too quickly for Sophie. Marc had called exactly twice since the last time they'd seen each other, both times to check in about the progress on the fundraiser. His tone had been casual and friendly, but he'd made no mention of seeing her. Instead, he'd talked about how busy he was with the trial and how sorry he was he couldn't help more as she planned the event. It was like listening to herself whenever a guy failed to get the hint that she wasn't interested.

Fuck him was becoming her standard line. Anytime she felt depressed about his rejection, she just took a deep breath and said, "Fuck him."

"Who are we fucking?" Jordan asked.

Sophie grinned. "No one. Unfortunately."

"Speak for yourself." Jordan was the current poster child for sexually-active-and-loving-every-second-of-it women everywhere. It made Sophie want to scratch her drowsy, I-was-up-all-night-screwing-two-hot-guys eyes out.

"Bitch."

Jordan laughed and continued arranging the chairs in rows.

Sophie had just finished stringing a line of lights around the stage when Marc walked in. As one of the night's eligible bachelors, he was dressed to the nines in a tuxedo. Sophie tried to ignore the parts of her body that stood up and took notice of how fucking hot he looked.

More than once, she'd wondered if he was putting distance between them as a way of keeping his options open for tonight. "Asshole," she muttered, praying she could summon the strength to play it cool.

Marc waved to her from the front door then made a beeline for the bar.

Great. On top of being an asshole, he was a coward, maybe even a drunk. She adjusted the microphone, doing a quick sound check while composing a list of unflattering descriptions for the attorney in her head.

Arrogant. Cocky. Annoying. Liar. Attractive. Funny. Smart.

Shit.

Stupid list.

She stepped off the stage as Marc approached. She took a deep breath and girded her loins, as Jayne—the romance-reading queen—liked to say.

"Here." Marc handed her a drink.

She took the glass without thinking. "What's this?"

"Some concoction Stephanie whipped up for me at the bar. It's called Bachelor's Bait." He wiggled his eyebrows at her suggestively.

"In case you failed to remember, I'm running this shindig tonight. I can't do that if I'm half-lit."

"Take a drink, princess. I can tell you're uptight. It might relax you a bit."

She narrowed her eyes. He had some nerve trying to tell her to do anything. He'd avoided her for almost a month. Gotten a freaking blowjob and then blown her off. "Listen, Marc, I don't appreciate—"

He kissed her before she could finish properly eviscerating him. "I'm sorry, Soph. More sorry than I can say."

"For what?"

"I've picked up the phone at least twenty times a day these past few weeks to call you, but every time I started to dial I got interrupted. My life has been a living hell— constant work and family issues. I spent four nights sleeping at the desk in my office."

"I thought you quit your job at the big law firm to avoid the all-work-and-no-play lifestyle."

Marc nodded. "I did. And for the most part, the move worked. Occasionally though, major things hit at the same time and I end up paying for it for a few weeks before they settle back down. Figures my work life would go to hell just as my personal life is starting to look up."

"Oh?" She tried to play coy. "What's going on in your personal life that's so special?"

He gripped her waist, pulling her closer. She stiffened, refusing to lean into him, regardless of how good he smelled. "You. I haven't been able to stop thinking about you and it's driving me nuts. I told myself I wouldn't call you again until I had time to see you, be with you, strip off all your clothes and have sex with you all night long."

She was weakening and it pissed her off. She wanted to stay mad, continue to play the indignant card. Rather than acknowledge his apology, she lifted the drink and took a big swig without thinking. The foul taste hit her hard.

Slapping her hand over her mouth, she forced herself to swallow before handing him the glass. "Holy. Crap. What the hell is in that?"

Marc shrugged. "I don't know. Something with gin. Looked like egg whites, maybe."

"Raw egg? Gross!"

Marc chuckled, taking the glass from her and putting it on the edge of the stage. He took her hand and she started to slap it away before realizing he wasn't trying to hold it—he was giving her something.

She looked down as he placed a huge wad of cash into her hand.

"What's that for?"

"It's five hundred dollars. I want you to bid on me."

She frowned. While his apology had gone a long way toward alleviating some of her anxieties and soothing a small part of her wounded pride, she wasn't quite ready to let him off the hook. "What if I don't *want* to bid on you? I happen to know there's a very hot optometrist coming tonight. I can totally see myself with him."

"No pun intended, I'm sure." Marc lifted her hand, closing her fingers over the money she was trying to return to him. "Bid on me, Sophie. Give me a chance to make things up to you. You won't be sorry. I promise."

She continued to hold his money out, but Marc shoved his hands in his pockets, refusing to accept it. "Even if I *were* to bid—and I'm not saying I'll bid on you—I have my own money to spend."

"I want to contribute to the charity, but obviously I don't

plan to buy a bachelor to do it. Throw my money in with whatever you'd intended to spend on me. I'm worth every penny." He gave her a cocky wink.

"Ugh. You are so annoying. I have work to do."

She started to walk away, but Marc pulled her back. Her traitorous body moved toward him, eyes drifting closed as he placed a soft kiss on her lips. Moving away an infinitesimal degree, he whispered to her, his lips brushing against hers as he spoke. "Put the high bid on me and our date starts tonight. I'm taking you back to my place. I'm going to unzip that sexy dress you're wearing and watch it fall to the floor. I've spent too many nights imagining how good it's going to feel to bury myself inside you. Once I get there, I'm not sure I'll ever want to leave again."

"What about the trial?"

"It ended today."

"Family drama?"

"Also resolved. Cancer scare with my mom. She got the all clear on the biopsy two days ago."

Sophie officially felt like shit for every bad thought she'd had about Marc. "Thank God for that."

"I'm going to keep you in my bed for days, weeks, maybe months."

She released a short, breathless laugh. "Big words. Sure you're up for it?"

He pressed their bodies closer together, letting her feel just how *up* he was. His erection brushed against her stomach, and she fought to restrain a groan. Her pussy was wet, throbbing, tired of being empty.

"I'm going to take you hard and fast the first time. I need

you that much. We'll be damn lucky if we make it to my bedroom. Hell, my house might be too far away."

Sophie's eyes remained closed, soaking in each sexy word. She'd wasted far too many hours fantasizing over him as well. She wanted every single thing he promised, but still, self-preservation held her aloof. "So that's my big date if I win? You're going to show me the inside of your bedroom?"

"Christ. I'll wine and dine you if you want. Buy you a fur coat, a condo, a kitten, anything. Just bid on me, Sophia. Put me out of my misery."

She expected to see more arrogance on his face. Instead, she saw pure, genuine need. Unable to resist, she closed the distance between them, initiating the kiss. She wasn't in the mood for gentle caresses. He'd lit a flame inside her in his office. Since then it had smoldered and grown. Tonight, an inferno raged.

His fingers tightened on her hips as she forced his lips apart with hers, dipping her tongue inside his mouth. Obviously he hadn't tried the vile drink Stephanie had made. He tasted like Scotch. It was delicious, sweet, heady.

"Ahem," came a voice next to them. "I think it's bad form to steal a bachelor before the auction."

Sophie and Marc parted. Stephanie stood next to them, gesturing toward the door. Several women were gathering outside, waiting to come in.

Marc's hand still rested on Sophie's waist. He stroked her with his thumb, drawing small circles that turned her on as much as his kisses. "I'll head upstairs to wait with the other bachelors. See you later, princess."

She heard the double meaning behind his farewell.

There was no doubt in her mind exactly how much of each other they'd be seeing. She glanced at his ass as he left.

Oh yeah. She intended to see it all.

"Don't make me throw a bucket of cold water on you," Stephanie threatened.

Sophie grinned, certain she looked like a lovesick fool. Shit, she felt like one.

"Thought you were mad at the asshole for not calling."

"He apologized."

Stephanie nodded slowly. "Sophie, I'm a little worried about you with this guy. I'm not sure I've ever seen you so..."

"Interested?" God knew she'd never spared a second glance for any of the men her father had deemed worthy of her time.

Stephanie shrugged. "I guess that works. I was sort of thinking you've fallen ass over tit for him."

Sophie laughed. "Christ, Steph. Only you could take a romantic phrase like head over heels and make it raunchy. And for your information, I'm not falling. I'm horny. Marc's offered the most promising proposition I've had for sex in a long time."

"Liar, liar, thong on fire. Pretend it's just sex if you want, but..." Stephanie paused. Her friend was never at a loss for words. "Just...be careful. Okay?"

Sophie appreciated the advice, praying she wasn't making a fool of herself. "I will."

"Soph," Jayne called out from across the bar. "Can I open the doors? The natives are getting restless."

She looked at the growing pack of women standing outside Books and Brew. Patricia had done an amazing job spreading the word. The event was certain to be standing room only. The bachelors had baited their hooks and now they just had to reel in the dough.

Sophie considered her own plans for one particular handsome bachelor. She'd prepared for this event for weeks. Now it was here and she wished it were over.

Her hand tightened on the money Marc had handed her, and she smiled.

Let the bidding begin.

CHAPTER FIVE

Marc pulled onto his street and glanced over at the passenger seat. Sophie had been uncharacteristically quiet since they'd left Books and Brew. He'd known walking into the event tonight that he owed her an apology. He'd never bungled the beginning of a relationship so badly.

Relationship. It had taken him nearly the entire month he and Sophie had been apart to admit that was what he wanted. He had thought she'd represented everything he'd spent most of his adult life trying to escape—family name, social status, pursuit of wealth. When he left the law firm, it was because he was sick of being surrounded by country-club mentalities, pursued by women who wanted him only because he had money. Marc had failed to tell Sophie his family was every bit as wealthy as hers. He'd let her believe he was a struggling attorney.

And she hadn't cared. She'd still called him, still come

around offering friendship and help to save the community center and the sweetest kisses he'd ever received.

He'd been worried earlier that he'd driven her away with his distance. There was a wicked streak inside her that hadn't been willing to let him off the hook easily. She'd set up the auction so that he'd followed the optometrist, who—much to his dismay—was extremely attractive. While Marc waited in the wings for his turn on stage, he'd had to watch Sophie and Patricia enter a bidding war for the hot doctor. Sophie had taken the bid all the way up to five hundred dollars before bowing out.

Then she'd made him sweat it out on stage, silently watching as two overeager cougars in the front row placed bid after bid on him. For a painful moment, he'd thought she was going to let one of the ladies win when the auctioneer said, "Going once, going twice..."

Sophie had finally raised her hand and slapped down all his money and a fair amount of her own to win the bid.

"Tired?" he asked. Her silence was slightly unnerving.

She looked at him and shook her head. "No. Not at all."

"Are you still mad at me, Soph?" If she was, why had she bid on him, accepted his arm after the auction and followed him to his truck, knowing where he intended to take her?

"No. I'm not."

Another short, unsatisfying answer. Marc turned into his driveway but didn't turn off the truck. His sixth sense was kicking. Something was up. "Do you want to come inside?"

She turned in the seat until she faced him. "I'm here, aren't I?"

"*Why* are you here?" The question slipped from his lips.

He hadn't meant to speak it aloud, but tonight felt like way more than a hookup to him. Suddenly he was feeling guilty about deceiving Sophie about his family, his financial situation.

"You said at Books and Brew that you couldn't stop thinking about me. I appear to be in the same boat. I want you, Marc. Physically, my body almost aches. But more than that, I *like* you. You're smart and funny and I'm sort of hoping this is headed somewhere—other than just your bed. Please tell me you're not playing me for a fool."

"Get out of the truck."

She blinked. "What?"

Marc didn't bother wasting time repeating himself. He crossed in front of the truck and pulled her door open. She started to step down, but he was too impatient. He gripped her hips as she exited, moving them slightly to the left then pushing her against the side of the vehicle. His lips found hers in an instant, and Sophie was there—waiting for him.

"You're not a fool. If anything, you're too damn good for me."

Then he kissed her hard, unable to find the words to convince her he was sincere. He was a lawyer, for God's sake. Words were his weapon. But tonight, right now, he couldn't find a single syllable that would fully express how he felt about her.

So he'd have to rely on instinct. He deepened the kiss, loving the way Sophie's arms gripped him tightly. She seemed to be driven by the same intense need, the hunger that begged for more. For everything.

His hands slipped lower, cupping her breasts. Sophie

groaned, the sound vibrating against his lips. He squeezed the generous flesh, slowly applying pressure until Sophie pulled away, gasping for air.

He studied her flushed face, her heavy-lidded eyes.

"Take me inside, Marc, or your neighbors are about to get one hell of a show."

He closed the passenger door and grasped her hand, tugging her quickly to the front door. The second he shut them inside, he pushed her against the door and kissed her again.

"You drive me crazy, princess. Fucking out of my mind."

She giggled softly. "I know the feeling. Bedroom?"

"Not sure I can make it." He reached down and grabbed her ass, tugging until she lifted her legs and wrapped them around his waist. Her short dress rode up, clearing the way for his pleasure. The door supported most of her weight as he pressed his covered cock against her pussy, slowly grinding against her twice, three times, letting her feel the extent of his need.

She tightened her legs around him. "God, Marc. Stop teasing me. Need you. Now."

Her words were a catalyst. He wanted to hold back, to take his time and do this right, but the reality was he wouldn't. Couldn't.

He shoved the thin strap of her thong aside and pushed two fingers inside her wet heat. Sophie's fingers dug into his upper arms almost painfully.

"Yes," she hissed. "Harder. Please. Harder..."

He began thrusting his fingers inside her, adding a third. She was tight, wet, ready. He stroked her clit with his thumb while his other hand supported her weight, gripping her ass. Holding on became harder as Sophie began gyrating, trying to force his fingers even deeper.

"Come for me, Soph. Let me see you come then I'll strip off these pants and push my cock inside you. I'll make you come again and again."

His dirty promise struck a nerve—the right nerve—and Sophie tensed, her muscles taut with the orgasm powering its way through her body. He held her steady, his fingers still buried inside her cunt. She was clenching against him tightly. He gritted his teeth, imagining that same gorgeous pulsing around his dick. He wouldn't last five minutes once he got inside her.

He slowly slipped his fingers out, relishing the small tremors that racked her body as her climax started to wane. Her legs unlatched from behind the small of his back, her feet falling none too gently to the floor. She found her balance as he reached for his belt, trying to unfasten his pants one-handed. His other hand lingered on her ass, steadying her.

Sophie's gaze drifted lower. She smiled when she saw him struggling, trying to move too quickly, too impatiently. She took mercy on him and reached out to help. Sophie's hands were steadier than his at the moment, so he left her to the task. He wanted to touch her—all of her—and see every bare, gorgeous inch.

While Sophie worked to divest him of his pants, he tackled the zipper at the back of her dress. They both worked rapidly. If Marc hadn't been in such pain, he would have laughed at their clumsy haste. Sophie shoved his slacks over his hips. He toed off his shoes then kicked off his pants and boxers. He still had his black socks on, but he wasn't about to take a break from stripping off her bra to remove them.

Sophie started unbuttoning his tuxedo shirt—he'd left the jacket in the truck—but he was finished waiting. He ripped the material open and shoved it off. To hell with the undershirt. It was going to have to stay.

"Sophie," he whispered before he bent to kiss her once more. Her breasts filled his hands nicely. He rubbed them roughly, enjoying her moans of desire. "Now."

"Yes."

He tugged her away from the door and gently guided her to the carpeted floor. Jesus. She'd commented on their "date" consisting of seeing his bedroom. He couldn't even get her that far.

He quickly stripped off her thong then reached for his pants. Retrieving a condom from his wallet, he soaked in the sight of Sophie as she lounged naked on his floor.

He took a deep breath, trying to steady himself, to get a grip—otherwise this was going to be over pretty damn fast. "I promised you wine and dinner."

She giggled. "All my dates give me wine and dinner. This is way better. I feel so sexy and hot right now. No one's ever wanted me so much. I could get used to this."

Marc smiled at her joke. "I think you're going to have to. You *are* sexy. Jesus. You're fucking gorgeous. And regardless of what the other jackasses in your past have done, I still owe you a meal."

"Fine. Then I want breakfast in bed."

"Done." He finished slipping on the condom then pushed her legs apart. Sophie reached up as he bent over her, pulling him closer for another long, lingering kiss.

As their lips danced, he placed his cock at the opening to her body and slowly pushed in.

Sophie gasped. "So good!"

"I'm sure I'm not as big as Chuck, but—"

Sophie pinched his hip. "I wouldn't be so sure of that. He was a big dick, but you're proving to be—"

He bit her shoulder then slid in farther as they both laughed softly.

Neither of them spoke again. Once Marc was seated to the hilt, he paused for a moment and lifted his head until he could see her face.

"Ready?"

She nodded. Her cheeks were pink from their earlier exertions, her hair was hanging in her face, her eyelids were heavy with sensuality and her lips were swollen from his nonstop kisses. In a word, she looked perfect.

Marc withdrew until just the head of his cock was nestled in her body, then he thrust again—harder, faster than before. Sophie raised her legs to his waist, granting him more room to move, allowing him to go deeper.

He watched as her eyelids drifted closed, her face the picture of pleasure.

So this is what complete and utter bliss feels like.

Soon he gave up trying to prolong the inevitable. This wasn't going to be a one-time deal or even a one-night stand. They'd perfect the longevity of the act later.

For now...

In and out he moved. Relentlessly. Without pause.

Both he and Sophie groaned, clinging to each other until they were sweaty, sticky messes, neither of them willing to stop.

Sophie squeaked when he hit a certain spot and his rhythm faltered.

"Holy shit! Right there. God, right there. Do that again," she urged.

He obliged, loving her much louder cries, the way she gripped his upper arms. Marc was close. So fucking close, but he wasn't going without her.

Lifting her legs, he placed her knees over his shoulders, opening her for the ultimate penetration. She screamed when he thrust again. Reaching down, he rubbed her clit, watching as she splintered, came apart. Her fingers clenched in his carpet as her pussy muscles clamped against his cock.

It was all he needed. Actually, it was too damn much. Marc pushed once, twice more as he came, come filling the condom while his body jerked.

"Fuck. Oh fuck, Sophie. God *damn*." His arms buckled beneath him. He went to his forearms, barely managing to hold himself above her.

Sophie was breathing hard. Her eyes remained shut for only a moment longer, then she opened them, capturing his with her bright blue gaze.

They stared at each other, neither of them bothering to speak. He wasn't sure if the quiet was due to a lack of breath or words. There didn't seem to be a way to accurately describe how amazing that was.

Once he'd regained some strength, Marc sat up. Sophie followed, looking around at their surroundings.

He'd taken her on the floor of the front foyer. They hadn't made it more than three steps inside.

"Nice house," she said at last.

Marc laughed. "Come on, princess." He rose and offered a hand to help her up. He was still wearing his black socks and the T-shirt he'd donned under his tuxedo shirt.

She took one look at him and giggled. He rolled his eyes and tugged her closer. "Want a tour of the place now or later?"

"I want a tour of your bedroom."

"Easily arranged." He grasped her hand and led her down the hallway toward the master bedroom. He loved his little ranch-style house with everything on one floor. He didn't stop once they'd crossed the threshold. He kept walking until they reached the bed then pulled back the comforter and sheets. He stripped his remaining clothes before picking up Sophie and tossing her on the middle of the mattress as she laughed.

He joined her on the bed. Sophie met him halfway, reaching for him without hesitance and they kissed again. It was a simple melding of the mouths, but it lasted forever. Marc couldn't resist. She smelled like strawberries, tasted like wine and her skin was as smooth as silk.

He caressed her back, her hips and waist. Let his fingers explore as he continued to worship her lips with his.

Sophie moaned softly when his fingers brushed her ass. He took the sound as an invitation. His cock thickened as Sophie shifted closer.

He gripped her ass in his palm, lightly squeezing. Sophie squirmed then lifted her leg over his hip. They lay on their sides, facing each other. Her new open position gave him plenty of room to explore. He dragged his fingers along the slit of her ass until he reached her anus. He wiggled his finger around the rosette as Sophie's hands surveyed his chest.

He was taken off guard when Sophie applied pressure to his chest, pushing him to his back. She came over him, straddling his hips.

She cradled his cock between her legs, moving just slowly enough to drive him out of his mind.

"You're killing me, Soph. If you want a ride, lift up and do it properly."

She gave him a wicked grin that said she liked tormenting him too much. She slowed her motions even more.

He closed his eyes and tried to ignore how good the heat of her pussy felt as she gave his dick the sexiest massage in history. He spread his legs and bent his knees, trying to give himself more leverage and her more room. He lifted his hips against her, forcing a deeper stroke, a longer rub.

Sophie leaned forward slightly. The new position brought her clit into the line of fire. She closed her eyes, but his gaze never left her face. Her sensuous assault teased every single one of his senses. He could smell her arousal, feel how hot and wet she was for him. Her rosy nipples had his mouth watering for a taste while her quick moans fueled his hunger. He imagined her face looked just like this whenever she gave herself pleasure. Marc vowed he would ask her to masturbate for him. He longed to watch her self-induced orgasms. If the look of almost-pain on her face was anything to go by, he suspected she was fairly close to that point right now.

They'd indulged in quick, passionate fucking earlier. Now Sophie was looking for a slow, sexy ride. He wasn't sure how much longer he could hold off. He'd done the dry-humping routine as a teenager but he'd never tried this wet-humping game Sophie was initiating him into.

Whatever it was, it was fucking hot. And yet...

His fingers tightened on her hips and before he could think about his actions, he reversed their positions. Sophie tumbled to her back as Marc crawled over her. Her legs parted, welcoming him. If she was annoyed at losing control, her face didn't show it. Instead, she raised her arms and pulled him down on top of her.

"I want to come on your breasts."

She smiled. "Okay."

"But first..." He moved lower, placing an innocent kiss on her clit. Her eyes started to drift shut once more, but he shook his head. "No. Watch me."

Her gaze found his just as he pressed his tongue inside her pussy.

"Oh God," she cried. Her hands tangled in his sheets as he tongue-fucked her. He'd only had a taste of her in his office that day, but his mouth had watered for more ever since.

Sophie's breathing accelerated, and he sensed she wanted to look away, but her gaze held steady. He opened her legs even farther, using his hands rather than words to position her. He wanted her completely open to him.

He glanced up as he nipped her clit, applying just

enough pressure to make it sting. Sophie didn't complain, didn't try to shove him away. Her hungry look solidified some suspicions that had formed after their brief sexual foray in his office. She liked to play and she was ready to push some limits.

Marc decided to see just how far she was willing to go. He moved lower, pressing his tongue around the rim of her anus. Sophie gasped, but once again she didn't pull away, didn't close her eyes. He licked the rosette until it was nice and wet, then he pushed a single finger in to the first knuckle.

"You said anal play was one of the kinky things you've tried."

She nodded.

"How far did you go?"

Her cheeks flushed and he grinned, loving the innocence that tinted her naughtiness.

"Just a finger."

"One finger?"

She nodded again.

"No toys? No cocks?"

She shook her head.

He pushed his finger deeper, watching her face carefully to make sure he didn't cause her any pain. He wouldn't venture farther than this tonight. Not without lube.

Once his finger was buried to the hilt, he pressed his mouth back to her pussy, shoving his tongue into the wet cavern as deep as it would go. Over and over he pushed his tongue inside, moving it in unison with the finger in her ass.

When he sensed she was getting close, he pushed the

button guaranteed to drive her over the edge. He rubbed her clit roughly with his free hand, loving the way Sophie's body went stiff just a split second before the trembling began. She came with her whole body, and it was a beautiful thing to watch.

Marc rose up on his knees and took his cock in his hand, stroking strong and hard as Sophie shivered in the aftermath of her orgasm, then he pulled his finger free of her body.

As she came to her senses, she reached out, ready to take over his hand job.

He shook his head. "No. Lift up your tits. Hold them for me."

She cupped her breasts, pushing the fleshy globes together then pinching her nipples. The image of her playing with herself had the desired effect. He bent closer, propping himself up with one hand as his other gripped and stroked his cock harder, faster, the head occasionally caressing soft flesh.

Sophie continued to play with herself, giving him the ultimate peep show.

"Holy shit, Sophie." His voice was too deep, his words sounding more like a growl. "Can't hold back."

Come shot from the tip of his cock, decorating Sophie's breasts with shiny droplets. She stilled, capturing every sticky strand.

Marc gasped for air, feeling light-headed from a lack of oxygen and the force of his climax. He thought the night couldn't get any better—until Sophie reached down to drag one finger through the come on her breast. She swirled it around her nipples, making them shine, then lifted the digit and stuck it in her mouth, sucking it clean.

"Shower?" she suggested.

He was wrong. The night had just gotten a *lot* better.

SOPHIE OPENED HER EYES SLOWLY, taking a moment to study her surroundings. She hadn't had the opportunity to see much of Marc's house last night.

She grinned. Besides the foyer floor, shower and this bed, she hadn't seen *any* of his home. His bedroom, now well lit by the sunshine streaming through the two windows, was surprisingly comfortable. There was a pile of unfolded laundry sitting on a chair, and his hamper looked as though it was in danger of exploding, but she supposed that was to be expected, given how busy he'd been the past few weeks.

She stretched lazily then winced. She'd gotten quite a workout last night. Marc had been insatiable. Of course, she had too. After their sexy shower, he'd wakened her in the middle of the night, taking her so gently she could have cried at the beauty of it. In one night, he'd given her passionate sex, raunchy play and then, just when she'd thought she had him figured out, he'd toned it down, making love to her as if she was the most precious thing on earth.

What a date.

Footsteps approached. She glanced toward the doorway in time to watch Marc walk in with a tray.

She smiled. "Breakfast in bed?"

"A promise is a promise."

She sat up, propping pillows along the headboard as Marc carefully set the tray over her lap. Sophie laughed when she spotted the apron he wore.

"*Grill or be grilled.* Is that lawyer humor?"

Marc shrugged. "I think it's sibling humor. My sister gave it to me for my birthday one year."

Sophie looked at the mountain of food on the plate in front of her and her eyes went wide. "I hope to hell you're planning to eat some of this with me. Otherwise, I think you can count on leftovers for lunch."

Marc stripped off the apron—he was naked underneath—and crawled back into bed. "There wasn't room on the tray for another plate." He picked up a fork and scooped up a pile of scrambled eggs. He directed the utensil to her mouth, so she took the bite. Then he helped himself to some.

"These are delicious," she said as she picked up a slice of crispy bacon. "You know how to cook."

Marc grabbed a piece of toast from the plate. "I'm thirty-five years old and I've never been married. Believe me, there's not enough takeout in the world to keep a man going that long."

Sophie could appreciate that truth. Growing up, her mother had made the family meals. Right after her death, Sophie and her father had gone through months of the Chinese-pizza-subs rotation, ordering out every night. Eventually, Sophie realized she was going to have to take charge in the kitchen or risk turning into an egg roll.

She picked up the orange juice and took a sip. "Hey, is there champagne in here?"

"Wine and dine, remember?"

She took another drink. "I love mimosas. Do you usually keep champagne in the house?" Marc didn't seem like a champagne drinker, so the idea that he had a bottle sort of screamed *player.*

He shook his head. "My sister gave me the bottle for Christmas. Told me to share it with someone I love on New Year's."

Sophie put the glass back on the tray. "Um, hate to break it to you, Marc, but you missed the holiday. New Year's was about seven months ago."

He polished off the last of the bacon. "I ended up going out with some friends over New Year's. Put the bottle in my wine rack and forgot all about it until this morning."

Sophie tried to batten down the girlie part of her that latched onto his sister's instructions. *Share it with someone you love.*

Play it cool, Soph.

"Well, it's perfect with OJ, so I'm glad you remembered it."

Marc studied her face. She wished she had inherited her father's knack for unreadable expressions. Her lawyer lover was too astute.

Marc gestured toward the tray. "You finished?"

She nodded. He put the tray on the floor by the bed.

"Sophie. I know it's way too soon in our relationship to talk about love and all that shit, but—"

"Shit?"

He grinned. "You know what I mean. The thing is, I've been around the block a few times. You don't make that trip without learning some things."

Sophie swallowed heavily, wondering where he was heading with this conversation.

"When I look at you...I see perfection. I'm a cocky know-it-all who doesn't have a romantic bone in his body, and I have no idea where this relationship is headed, but I'm pretty sure I'm going to fall for you."

"You are?"

Marc moved closer, cupping her face in his hands. His expression was far too serious for the fun-loving man she'd gotten to know. "Yeah. I'm warning you. I'm going to fall in love with you, Sophie. If you aren't looking for a relationship, a boyfriend, I'd like you to tell me now before things go too far."

Leave it to Marc to lay all the cards on the table. Then she recalled Stephanie's warning. "Actually, I've already been accused of falling for *you*. Might be nice not to make the trip alone."

A huge smile covered his face. Sophie couldn't resist leaning closer to kiss him. He accepted her embrace then deepened it. They'd spent hours last night just kissing and yet, Sophie still wanted more.

"Anybody ever tell you how sexy you look in the morning?" he murmured against her lips.

She shook her head, her hand instinctively reaching up to touch her hair. She'd fallen asleep with wet hair after their shower last night. There was no way she looked like anything less than a disaster. "Perjury is a crime."

"Didn't realize I was under oath." Marc grasped her hand, pulling it away from her hair. "But even if I was, I'd still say the same."

"And you think you're not romantic."

He laughed as she sighed softly. Damn. Suddenly the idea of falling for Marc seemed like an understatement. Stephanie was right. She was ass over tit and showing no signs of straightening herself out.

Marc pushed her to her back, climbing over her. She opened her legs for him, the reaction coming so naturally already.

He belonged there. She belonged *here*.

It was time Sophie put aside all her feelings of doubt and did something that didn't come naturally to her.

She took a leap of faith.

———

CHAPTER SIX

Sophie walked into Books and Brew feeling like a million bucks.

"You're late," Stephanie called out from behind the bar.

"I don't care. You're lucky I'm here at all."

Jayne's head popped up from behind a bookshelf. "Hot damn. You had sex."

Sophie grinned and nodded. "I did and it was incredible, amazing, un-fucking-believable."

Elias, one of their regulars, looked up from the newspaper he was reading and grinned. "Good for you, Sophie," he said, before returning his attention to local happenings.

Sophie looked over and noticed Stephanie texting. She rolled her eyes. "Jeez. Calling Jordan down again?"

Stephanie looked at her with one eyebrow raised. "She'll kill me if I don't."

Sophie placed her purse behind the bar and grabbed an

apron. Nothing could bring her down today. She was on cloud nine, flying a hundred feet above the ground.

Jordan appeared at the bottom of the stairs and made a beeline for the bar. "I want to hear *all* about the sex, but first—you did it!"

Sophie frowned, confused. "I know I did it. I thought that's why you were rushing down here. To hear the dirty details."

"No," Jordan said, laughing. "Not Marc. The *fundraiser*. You raised the funds! We hit the goal!"

Sophie's jaw dropped. She'd suspected last night that they had done well, but in her heart, she knew they were still short. Jordan, ever the bookkeeper, had offered to stay late to count the money. Sophie had expected bad news, so she'd decided to escape with Marc and postpone hearing the dire results until today. "How? I was sort of counting in my head, Jordan. I know I'm not great at math but I'm not *that* bad. We didn't hit it."

"Gabriel was true to his word. He matched what we made, but you're right, it still wasn't enough. So he made some phone calls. He didn't have any luck. Then, first thing this morning, Rich Gregory called to say someone had stepped forward and covered the remaining shortfall. The center is saved!"

"Who?"

Jordan shrugged. "We don't know. Rich said the donation was made anonymously. Besides, who cares who? You did it!"

Stephanie and Jayne had come over as Jordan shared the good news. They exchanged hugs and high-fives. "I can't believe it," Sophie said over and over.

"So enough of that. I want to hear about last night. Was he worth the money you paid?" Stephanie asked with a wink.

Sophie snorted. "Real nice, Steph. It's not like I was hiring him to be some sort of paid escort."

Jayne leaned closer. "Was it romantic? Marc strikes me as a candlelight-and-roses kind of guy."

Stephanie sighed dramatically. "Real life is not like those goddamn regency romance novels you read, Jayne."

Jayne held up her hand in talk-to-it fashion while keeping her attention focused on Sophie.

Sophie smiled. "He definitely has romantic tendencies. He brought me breakfast in bed this morning."

Jayne smirked at Stephanie. "See."

Stephanie never went down without a fight. "I saw you two when you left here. Twenty bucks says you never made it out of the truck before you jumped each other."

Technically, Stephanie was wrong. Sophie had definitely gotten out of the truck before Marc had shoved her against it and kissed her so hard her eyes rolled into the back of her head. "We made it out of the truck."

"Mmm-hmm," Stephanie hummed. "*How far* out of the truck?"

"We had sex on the floor right inside his front door."

Jordan laughed. "Jesus. I bet that was hot."

Sophie couldn't contain her glee. "It was the hottest sexual experience of my life. I've never had a guy want me that badly."

"And the sex was *that* good?" Jordan asked.

Sophie sighed. "Heaven on earth."

Jayne shook her head. "Damn. That's three of you getting laid now. I'm starting to feel like the odd guy out."

Sophie wrapped her arm around Jayne's shoulders. "Your day is coming, Jayne. I promise."

Jayne crossed her arms. "Yeah, well. I hope it comes while I'm still young enough to try some of the more interesting poses in the *Kama Sutra*."

Stephanie's gaze jerked to Jayne. "Since when do you read the *Kama Sutra*?"

Jayne blushed. "Uh...a friend loaned it to me."

"What friend?" Stephanie asked.

"None of your business." Jayne turned and walked back to the box of new books she'd been shelving when Sophie walked in.

Sophie's brows rose at Jayne's unexpected spunkiness.

"Who the hell gave her the *Kama Sutra*?" Stephanie repeated.

Jordan and Sophie both shrugged.

"Oh shit. Elias asked for another drink ten minutes ago." Stephanie swiftly walked behind the bar to pour Elias his usual Scotch.

Sophie followed. "I'll take it to him."

Picking up the glass, she crossed the room. "Hi, Elias."

"Hello, Sophie. It sounds like you had a good night."

Sophie grinned. "It was the best night of my life."

"High praise. Marc Garrett is a very lucky man."

Sophie started to reply, but something outside caught her eye. "Crap," she muttered as she absentmindedly placed Elias' drink on the table before him.

"Something wrong?"

"My dad's limo just pulled up out front."

Elias followed her gaze to the front windows. "I see."

Sophie glanced back at Elias. He'd been Books and Brew's most faithful customer since they'd opened the doors. He'd also become a friend. "I can tell by your tone you know what's going on. With the community center?"

Elias nodded. "Jayne filled me in on the details. Preying on my sympathy as part of her plea to get me to participate in that auction last night."

Sophie had been shocked when she'd seen Elias' name on the list of eligible bachelors—until she'd heard it was Jayne who'd convinced him. Elias seemed to have a soft spot for her shy friend. She also knew for a fact that Jayne was harboring a huge crush on the science professor as well. "As I recall, yours was one of the highest bids of the night." Unfortunately, Jayne wasn't the winner.

Elias shook his head. "Don't remind me. My 'date' has already called twice to confirm the details. Something tells me I'm in for a long night."

Sophie smiled. "You're a good sport." She glanced back toward the door nervously, just in time to see her father step out of the limo. Her first instinct was to flee, to run out the back door.

"Be brave, Sophie."

"What?" she asked, looking at Elias once more.

"You've already done the hard part. You fought Goliath and won. Don't belittle that victory by hiding now."

Much as she hated to admit it, Elias was right. The bell above the door jingled, announcing Dad's arrival. She stood up straighter as she turned to face him.

Dad crossed the room, nodding a silent hello to Elias. The greeting was returned.

"Sophie. Could I have a moment of your time?" Dad asked.

She nodded, hoping her legs—which suddenly felt like Jell-O—would support her. She followed Dad to a quiet table in the corner. It was only as she took her seat that she realized he'd called her "Sophie".

"Rich Gregory called me this morning," Dad started.

Sophie didn't reply. Sounded as if the chairman had spent most of his morning on the telephone.

"He said that you'd raised the funds to save the center."

She tried to read his voice or his face. Hell, she'd take *any* hint as to how he was handling the news that she'd defeated him, but—as always—her father was impassive. "The fundraiser last night surpassed all of our expectations."

"Yes," her father said. "I read about your bachelor auction in the paper this morning. I have to say, Sophie, I'm a bit disappointed and more than a little hurt."

It was the first time in ages she heard a tinge of the man her father used to be, before the loss of her mother, before work had consumed him and turned him into an emotionless shell of his former self.

She resisted the urge to apologize. For years she'd tried to please her dad. Agreeing to go on the dates he set up for her, serving as his hostess at parties, playing the role of a dutiful daughter. She'd done it all even as he'd slipped further and further away from her with each passing day. "I told you I would do everything in my power to save the center. I didn't do any of this behind your back."

"I know. That's not what I meant—I'm upset that you didn't think to include me as one of the bachelors. It's not as easy as you might think for a man my age to meet available women. God knows I'm not about to try one of those online dating service things."

Sophie's jaw dropped as shock hit. She glanced around the bar, trying to decide if she was actually awake.

"Close your mouth, Soph, or you'll catch flies."

She laughed, the sound bursting out of her before she could call it back. Marc had said the exact same thing to her once.

"You would have participated in the auction?"

Dad nodded. "I would have."

"But why? Why would you take part in something that would hurt you financially? What happened to 'it's not personal, it's business'?"

Dad reached out and took her hand. She swallowed heavily, trying to dislodge the lump created by the sweet gesture. "I was wrong. I felt terrible after our disagreement. I walked over to the mantel and forced myself to look at those pictures. Did you know I haven't looked at them once since your mother died?"

Sophie frowned. "Then why leave them there? You've remodeled the whole house. Why keep the pictures if they bothered you so much?"

Dad shrugged. "I couldn't do it. Couldn't put them away. But when I stood there remembering those days, I realized I've put *you* away. Tucked you over to one side because it hurt too much to..." He squeezed his eyes shut and rubbed his brow. When he looked at her again, he seemed to have composed himself. "Please tell me it's not too late for me to make things right with you again. I miss you, Sophie."

As she looked into the eyes of her beloved father, a light went on. "You were the anonymous donor, weren't you?"

Her father gave her a noncommittal smile.

Sophie was torn between laughter and tears. Her beloved daddy was back—and he'd saved the community center for her.

There was so much they needed to say to each other, but Marc walked into Books and Brew before she could speak. The look of concern on his face when he saw her sequestered in the corner with her dad was immediate. She raised her hand to wave and smiled so he'd know everything was okay.

"You know Marc Garrett?" Dad asked.

Sophie nodded. "Yes." She wasn't sure how much more to say.

"I think I understand now. *He* was your source. That's how you knew so many details about the center's financial troubles that day you came by the house."

She bit her lip, unwilling to risk unleashing her dad's anger on Marc.

"Are the two of you dating?" he asked.

She wasn't sure "dating" was a word she could use. Truth was, they'd yet to go out on a proper date, though he had certainly wined and dined her. Still, it was an easier explanation than admitting to her father they'd spent hours last night fucking each other into oblivion. "Yes. We are."

Dad smiled. "He's a good match for you. I couldn't have found a better suitor myself."

Sophie tilted her head, wondering if she'd heard him correctly. "Really? You've been setting me up with rich, snotty guys for years. You can't seriously sit here and say you're okay with me dating a dirt-poor free-aid attorney."

Dad's smile dimmed, but before he could say anything, Marc approached the table.

"Hi, Soph," he said cautiously. "Mr. Kennedy."

Dad stood up and proffered his hand, which Marc shook. "Call me Jasper. I understand you're dating my little girl."

Marc glanced down at her. Sophie felt her face flush as the familiar twinge of fear crept through her. Their relationship was still too new, too fragile in her mind. How long would it take for her to believe it was all real?

"That's right," Marc said, smiling warmly. He held out his hand and she took it, rising. "Sophie's my girlfriend."

Sophie giggled at the way he stressed *girlfriend*, as if he was trying the word on for size. She noticed her father studying her face carefully. She wasn't sure what he saw reflected there, but whatever it was seemed to set his mind at ease.

"I'm glad to hear it. Any chance you'll eventually open up a West Coast branch of your father's firm? I suspect the Garrett name would find success in any city."

"The Garrett name?" Sophie asked, feeling slightly uneasy.

Dad looked at her quizzically. "The Garrett law firm is one of the most prestigious and profitable organizations on the East Coast."

Sophie turned her attention to Marc as this new fact about her *boyfriend* fell into place. "You're rich?" she asked.

Marc didn't reply at first, then he cleared his throat uneasily. "Technically, my *family* is rich."

Her father, not catching the undertones in their conversation, chuckled. "Semantics, my dear boy. Filthy rich, I'd say."

"Filthy rich," she repeated, her gaze narrowing.

This time her tone alerted her father there was something wrong. "Well, I mean, I guess I could be overestimating his family's wealth or..."

Marc's guilty expression said that her father's guess had been dead-on. "No, I don't think you were," she said softly.

"Sophie—" Marc began.

She held up her finger to stop him. "Wait."

She turned to her father. Too many things were falling in on her at once. She needed to deal with the men in her life one at a time. "Dad, it's not too late."

Dad's brow creased for a moment then cleared when he realized what she was saying. His smile grew. "Thank God. I thought I'd lost you for good. I love you, Soph. That never stopped, never went away. I just lost my way and—"

"I know." She took a step closer, walking into her father's embrace. He hugged her tightly. The strength of his arms and the memories of being held like this as a child crept up on her. She felt a tear trickle down her cheek. "I love you too," she whispered against his chest.

Dad pulled away and pressed a kiss to the top of her head. "Come by for lunch tomorrow? I have a meeting arranged with Rich Gregory about future plans for the community center. He and I are hoping we can convince you to spearhead some of the programs."

For years, she'd resisted her life and the path she'd seemed destined to walk, feeling as though it wasn't a worthy calling. Now she understood she had a knack for organizing charity events, planning parties, fundraising. And more than that, it was something she enjoyed. "I'd like that."

"You are so much like your mother."

Her father's compliment filled Sophie's heart until she feared it would burst.

Dad said his goodbyes to her, and Marc and she watched as he walked to his limo.

Once he was gone, she turned her attention to Marc—the millionaire-pauper lawyer.

"Sophie, I can—"

She ignored him, looking over her shoulder toward the back of the bar. "Come with me."

Marc looked as if he wanted to insist she hear him out, but instead he followed when she led him to the storeroom. Once they were inside, she shut the door. The small space reminded her of the coat closet.

Marc's face resembled that of a man standing before the firing squad. It took all the strength she had not to laugh.

"Are you going to give me a chance to explain?"

She shook her head. "I don't care."

"Goddamn it, Soph! I know we haven't been seeing each other that long, but I think I've at least earned the right to—"

"I don't care," she said louder. "I don't care about your family's prestigious name or law firm or money. I know why you didn't tell me. Jesus, Marc. Do you really think I don't get it?"

He fell silent. She could tell he was still uncertain.

"I'm actually a bit jealous of your bravery. I never for a moment considered moving away from Portland, moving someplace where Jasper Kennedy's name meant nothing. Instead, I've lived here my entire life, allowing my dad to set me up with eligible men because the guys I would have *liked* to date were too intimidated by my father's wealth to ask me out."

Marc frowned. "You really don't care?"

She shook her head. "Not about the money. I mean, I don't want to be judged because of how much I stand to inherit, so how can I subject you to the same thing without being a gigantic hypocrite? However, you *do* owe me an apology—a big one—for not giving me the same consideration when we first met."

Marc's shoulders sagged. "You're right. I was a huge dick."

She laughed. "Wow. I stand corrected. You and Chuck don't have anything in common. You actually get it."

Marc shoved his hands in his front pockets, looking miserable, worried. "I'm really sorry, Sophie. And I don't blame you if you don't feel like accepting my apology this time. I'm saying those words to you way too often."

She tilted her head. "Is there anything else you're hiding from me? Need to make amends for?"

"No. I can't think of anything. At the moment."

She stepped closer. "Good."

"So we're okay?"

"I'd say we're a little better than okay, wouldn't you? Last night was..." She let Marc fill in the blanks, helping him along as she dragged her fingers along his chest seductively.

Marc released a long, loud sigh of relief that made her happier than she thought possible. He'd been more nervous than she'd realized. The idea that he was afraid of losing her touched her heart.

He wrapped his arms around her, hugging her so tightly it took her breath away. Her stomach brushed his erection.

She pulled away and glanced down. "Seriously? We ran

a damn marathon last night and this morning. You can't honestly..."

He grasped her hand, rubbing it along the front of his cargo pants and distracting her. "I told you before. It's these short skirts you wear."

He turned her away from him, and together they took a step closer to the door. Marc turned the lock on the knob then hit the light switch. They were plunged into absolute darkness.

Something about losing the sense of sight notched up Sophie's arousal. Her other senses kicked into overdrive.

"I'm afraid this isn't going to take very long. I've been hard since you left my house this morning. I swear to God, you're better than a dose of Viagra."

"Romantic fool," she teased. She started to laugh, but the sound quickly morphed to a gasp when Marc raised her skirt and slapped her ass. The burn of his hand against her sensitive flesh felt far too good. "Do that again," she whispered.

Marc repeated the slap on her other ass cheek then placed his hand on her back, subtly urging her to bend forward. Sophie pressed her hands against the door, tilting at the waist. The obvious acquiescence spurred Marc to action.

She heard the rasp of a zipper, the tearing of a wrapper, felt the head of his cock travel along her slit.

He hadn't lied. He was rock-hard, thick and ready. She felt him slide easily along her slick pussy and realized she was more than prepared to take him in herself.

"You're wet."

She nodded before realizing he couldn't see the gesture. Reaching back, she tried to halt his teasing rubs, to force his cock inside her body.

Marc brushed her hand aside.

"Stop screwing around." Her voice betrayed her hunger.

"I haven't even started screwing around yet."

She tried to grasp his cock again, but Marc anticipated the move, was there waiting for her. Gripping both of her wrists, he pulled them to the small of her back, holding them together with one hand. With the other, he placed three more hard, fast slaps on her ass.

She squirmed, twisted, seeking the relief only his cock could provide. Marc's grip tightened and Sophie groaned. God. She'd never been so turned-on in her life.

"Hold still," he demanded.

He may as well ask her to fly to the moon. She was capable of neither. He spanked her again and she trembled with need.

"Please," she whispered, pride be damned. The entire experience was driving her out of her mind. The darkness, the spanking, her immobile wrists. It was as if Marc had a direct line to her dirtiest fantasies.

"You like being controlled. Forced."

It wasn't a question. And he didn't sound turned off by that insight.

"Shit, Soph. Do you have any idea how hot that is?"

She forced herself to take deep breaths—air in through the nose, out from the mouth, in through the nose...

The head of his cock touched her anus and she shivered, wishing he'd shove the damn thing inside her—anywhere inside her.

"I'm stopping by the store as soon as I leave here and buying lube. I'm going to fuck this pretty little ass tonight."

"Yes," she whispered. He ran his free hand along the

heated cheeks. She stretched up on her toes, trying to invite more of that delicious stroking. Instead, he moved his hand and gathered a handful of her hair. Tightening his grip, he used it to pull her back to standing.

The vicious yank had her juices flowing. She'd never felt so wet. He moved them forward until her chest was flat against the door.

"You're my captive," he mumbled, his deep voice driving her fantasy into an entirely new realm.

"God!" she gasped. "Marc." Every word he spoke was pure magic, setting off sparks in parts of her body that had never known arousal until this moment. Her stomach clenched in anticipation, her nipples ached, her scalp tingled.

Marc nipped at her earlobe. "When you get to my place tonight, we're going to expand on this. I'm going to tie you to my bed, blindfold you, spank your ass and withhold your orgasm until you're begging for it, promising me anything and everything until I let you come."

"Please." She was begging him *now*, though she wasn't sure if it was his cock or his dirty promises that she wanted more.

Marc pulled her hands away from her back, placing them against the door, palms flat. "Keep them there. Don't move them."

Before she could respond, he grasped her hips, dragging them back until she was bent over once more.

Then, finally, he gave her exactly what she wanted. And then some. He shoved in to the hilt with one powerful thrust. The strength of it would have propelled her face-first into the door if her hands hadn't been there to hold her back. He didn't relent, didn't give her a chance to become accustomed to him. They'd proven last night and this morning that they fit perfectly.

He fucked her hard, just as he'd promised. When he reached around to touch her clit, Sophie cried out loudly.

Marc chuckled, then his other hand crept up, covering her mouth. "Quiet, Soph, or everyone in the bar will know what's going on in here."

Despite his comment, he continued to thrust, taking her to the point where she didn't give a damn who heard. His hand, silencing her, added to the illusion of being his captive. It brought her over hard.

Marc kept her mouth covered as her moans grew louder. Her climax ravaged through her. She'd only begun to come back to her senses when Marc came as well.

She loved the way his hand tightened on her hip as he climaxed. Though they'd only been together a few times, she was already becoming accustomed to his tells, the little hints that told her he was on the verge of losing control.

Those things made her feel even closer to him, and again, she was amazed by how quickly their relationship was progressing. He'd told her this morning he was going to fall in love with her. Now, though she knew it was too soon to say the words aloud, she had to admit he'd already staked a rather large claim on her heart.

Her future—with her handsome bachelor—had never looked so promising or so bright.

• • •

THERE IS STILL one Books and Brew lady looking for love. Are you ready for Jayne's story? Screaming O is available now.

HAVE YOU TRIED THEM ALL? If not, be sure to pick up all the Cocktales! The drinks are already poured and waiting for you.

Party Naked

Screwdriver

Bachelor's Bait

Screaming O

Party Naked

Cocktales, book 1

It's hate at first sight when hot cop Jarod gives cynical bartender Stephanie a ticket. So when Jarod finds himself in her bar that same evening working undercover, things go south quickly. An impromptu kiss--to keep Steph from blowing his cover--turns into a sizzling one-night stand.

Stephanie escapes the next morning, but Jarod isn't about to let her go. He wants the sexy woman back in his bed and she's more than worth the chase.

He'll even pull out the cuffs if necessary.

Party Naked - Available now

Screwdriver

Cocktales, book 2

Jordan spends way too much time fantasizing about her landlord, but she's in Gabriel's "just friends" column. She's prepared to pine forever—until she meets Casey. The handyman is sexy, handsome, charming...and Gabriel's best friend. Suddenly her wicked fantasies are porntastic times two.

Casey thinks it's time his billionaire bestie, Gabriel, gets off the bimbo train. The perfect woman for his friend? Jordan. The plan? Make Gabriel jealous by dating Jordan himself.

And it works. A little too well. Now they both want her. So....fight? Or share?

Screwdriver - Available now

Screaming O

Cocktales, book 4

Elias has resisted his attraction to Jayne, assuming his dominance in the bedroom would send her running for the hills. Alone in a snowstorm, Elias tests the waters and is blown away by Jayne's innate submissiveness. Ice play? Bondage? Flogging? Bring it on.

Soon it's no longer a question of whether or not Elias should pursue Jayne. She's made for him, and this determined alpha male will stop at nothing until he's claimed her —completely.

Screaming O - Available NOW.

ABOUT THE AUTHOR

Virginia native Mari Carr is a New York Times and USA TODAY bestseller of contemporary romance novels. With over two million copies of her books sold, Mari was the winner of the Romance Writers of America's Passionate Plume award for her novella, Erotic Research. She has over a hundred published works, including her popular Wild Irish and Compass books, along with the Trinity Masters series she writes with Lila Dubois.

Follow Mari:
www.maricarr.com
mari@maricarr.com

Join her newsletter so you don't miss new releases and for exclusive subscriber-only content.

www.ingramcontent.com/pod-product-compliance
Lightning Source LLC
Chambersburg PA
CBHW021003180726
47993CB00017B/659